The Lost Village

by Geoffrey Sleight

The sea is as near as we come to another world.

Anne Stevenson

CHAPTER 1

IT WAS nearly two hundred years ago when the coastal fishing village of Coatehaven dramatically collapsed into the sea.

Most of the inhabitants perished in the massive landfall. Only a few survived to live the remainder of their days in painful disability.

The terrible event was long past when Adam Collins bought the village's last remaining cottage. It stood just a short distance from the cliff edge, and had narrowly survived by being set slightly back from the main community. An overgrown, narrow cobblestone road leading from it once linked into Coatehaven high street.

Over time the remnants of the destroyed village had long since been removed from the shale beach below the cliff, and re-used by locals for building material. The sea claimed the rest of its new domain.

For the latest arrival to this part of England's north Norfolk coast, the remaining cottage was the start of a strange encounter with ghosts from that fateful past.

Adam joined a pharmaceuticals company in his early twenties, and his outstanding talent for selling was rewarded in him rising to executive level within a few years. But the pressures of work and overseas travel were intense. Now aged forty-five, his doctor had advised him to reduce his frantic pace of life, or if not he would die prematurely from a heart attack.

Adam had saved a considerable sum from high earnings, and the health warning led him to reconsider his lifestyle. He left his job and decided to pursue an interest from earlier times to become an artist, with particular liking for seascapes. The cottage by the sea fitted perfectly into the plan. The property had recently become vacant after an elderly woman who'd lived there for many years died. The woman had claimed seeing ghosts in the property, but that was a fact unknown to Adam.

Major players in Adam's life were wife, Josie, with teenage son and daughter, Liam and Olivia. He'd met and married Josie in a whirlwind romance on holiday in Rome, when they were in their late twenties. She ran a successful beauty salon business in the couple's home town of Guildford, to the south west of London.

But Adam's work and travel kept him constantly away from home. They had finally separated five years earlier, though he continued to pay fully for the children's upkeep and saw them as often as he could. There was no bitterness between the couple. They'd just diverged on different paths.

As he drove to the cottage from his central London flat in Notting Hill, it ran through his mind the property and seaside setting would be an ideal place for his children to spend enjoyable holidays there with him.

The pressures of his former life had blinded him to the really important elements of living. It felt like a heavy curtain opening and bright light illuminating the darkness that had blotted out his creative ambition. The old cottage was in need of extensive renovation, but he'd work on that as well as pursuing art.

Nearing the property along narrow country lanes in the blue Transit van he'd bought specially to carry equipment and provisions, Adam felt refreshed seeing sheep and cows grazing in the surrounding pastures. Ahead he caught sight of the glittering sea beyond the cliffs that ran close to the cottage.

The shell of another old cottage that had survived the landfall stood about a hundred yards from his own, but it had been abandoned many years earlier, the roof now collapsed and the windows gaping open to the elements. Surrounding it was a high wire safety fence. Adam's cottage was hardly pristine, numerous slate roof tiles missing and dark discoloured patches on the flint stone walls.

There were no other nearby properties in this remote part of the countryside.

Adam turned off the overgrown cobblestone road running past the cottage, parking on the gravelled frontage with low stone walls bordering each side. Now disused, the road outside linked into another one just in front of the property, leading directly ahead towards the old village of Coatehaven. Only a couple of hundred feet remained of this former horse and cart highway, barely visible under moss and grass, and ending abruptly at the cliff edge.

Exiting the vehicle he stretched his arms, gazing at the wonderful view of the sea and the cliffs curving away on each side into the distance. It felt like he'd arrived in paradise. After enjoying the view for a few more minutes, he began unloading the van.

Gripping a portable art easel under one arm, and carrying a travel bag in the other hand, he approached the front door. It was badly in need of less artistic painting with brown paint flaking from the woodwork.

"Welcome to Coatehaven," a voice came from behind. Adam stopped and turned back. Standing near the frontage was an elderly man in a white smock and bucket hat.

"Thank you," Adam returned the welcome, surprised by the man's clothing. It was the type of outfit worn by rural workers a very long time ago he thought. But then he'd moved to a place where things didn't change so rapidly, unlike the urban life he knew. Maybe it was still normal wear here.

The man approached and Adam could see crow's feet lines hugging the sides of his eyes in a weathered face largely covered by grey beard.

"I take it you know about the village that once stood beyond there," the man pointed towards the cliff.

"Yes, I've heard," Adam replied.

"Strange events can happen here. Don't be fooled by things that seem impossibly real," the man warned him. Adam watched as he turned and walked away, taking the cobblestone road leading towards the cliff edge and getting dangerously close to the drop.

Adam downed the easel and bag to run after him, fearing his eyesight might be dimmed with age and that he'd topple over the edge. But in that same moment a sea mist rose from the cliff face, spreading out and obscuring the man from view. Adam approached with caution, hoping he might be able to see his outline and guide him away from danger. Then as rapidly as it came, the mist dissolved. The man was gone. And no sign of him on the surrounding plain.

Adam carefully peered over the cliff edge down at the shale beach a few hundred feet below to see if he'd fallen. He'd heard no cry and as far as he could tell there was no body in view. A couple walking along the shore would probably have seen anyone fall he thought.

He walked back to the cottage beginning to wonder if he'd imagined the encounter. The man had seemingly disappeared into thin air, or mist as it happened. An encounter that seemed impossibly real.

Reaching for the key in his jeans pocket, Adam opened the front door and entered, placing the easel and bag down in the hallway.

The place was in need of serious updating. The walls of the hallway browned with age and the bare wood stairway worn into dips from countless feet using it over the years. A door to the left led into the kitchen. An old metal cooking range dominated the room with a work counter and crockery cabinet alongside which seemed suitable candidates for the refuse tip.

On the opposite side of the room a rotting sash window overlooked the front of the cottage, with a deeply scored ceramic sink, cold water tap and warped wooden draining board beneath it.

Adam knew from an earlier visit there was no gas or electricity supply, and the rundown state of the place allowed him to cash buy the property at a knock down price from the previous owner's son. But there was a log store at the back of the cottage to fuel the cooking range. Modern power was another 'to do' on Adam's renovation list. In the meantime LED lanterns would provide night light for him.

The living room was empty save for a wooden table and chairs left behind. Windows looked out to the front and back with a door to the side of the rear window leading into the yard, bordered by rotting wood fences.

Upstairs the front window of the main bedroom overlooked a magnificent view of the cliffs and sea into the distant horizon. An inspiring view to wake up to thought Adam as he turned to the metal bedstead bearing a thin mattress. They were also left by the previous owner at Adam's request. Of course he planned to buy a proper bed, but for now he'd lay the sleeping bag he'd brought with him on the mattress. More comfortable than bedding on the floor.

The second bedroom was empty, but that would be furnished so the children could visit for seaside breaks. The small bathroom was completely insufficient for modern needs. A badly stained toilet with a pull chain, stone sink with one cold tap and a metal bath with rust holes in the base. For the time being Adam would body and hair wash at the kitchen sink, using hot water boiled on the range.

After unpacking, he fired up the cooking range with logs from the store to heat a ready meal, and boiled water for coffee in a whistling kettle on the hot plate. Wi-Fi connection was not possible and the phone signal touch and go. Mostly gone. But this venture back into the old world way of living felt strangely refreshing to him. A retreat from modern life.

Settling in the living room that evening on a cantilever easy chair he'd brought along, Adam read some books on drawing and painting before retiring to bed.

It was ten o'clock when he made his way up the stairs to the bedroom, tired but happy with the new found freedom. Placing a lantern on a plastic drawer unit he'd brought for his clothes, he undressed, climbed into the sleeping bag on the bedstead mattress and switched off the light.

Something woke him from his peaceful sleep. He had no idea of the time. It must have been several hours since he'd settled down. Moonlight streamed through the uncurtained window. What had woken him?

Adam got out of the sleeping bag and went to the window. The light of the moon created a silvery path on the sea stretching towards the horizon. The scene looked beautifully serene. Perhaps the inexplicable power of nature had woken him to witness the view. Maybe inspire him to paint it at some point.

Then his eyes caught sight of a figure outside the cottage standing on the cobblestone road. It wore a smock and bucket hat, reminding Adam of the man who'd welcomed him with an oblique warning on his arrival. What was he doing standing in front of the cottage in the middle of the night?

The figure looked up at the bedroom window, appearing to shake his head in some kind of repeated warning. It must have been the same man he'd seen earlier, but his face was silhouetted from view in the moonlight behind.

Quickly dressing, Adam rushed downstairs and opened the front door. There was no-one in sight. He walked out to the cobblestone road. Still no-one in sight along its length.

Returning to the bedroom, he tried to make sense of his visitor. Maybe the man was a local oddity. Eccentric. Wandered the area night and day. And those peculiar clothes from another era? He seemed harmless enough though. Adam climbed back into his sleeping bag, puzzling the event for a while before settling to sleep again.

Over the next few days he spent time sketching sea-scapes from the clifftops along the coastline. The May weather held good with few clouds obscuring the sun. His sense of happiness and well-being soared.

On the third evening of his stay, he spent a few hours at the easel in the living room creating an oil painting from one of his sketches, showing surf waves breaking on a bay below that he felt captured the peaceful setting.

Before going to bed, Adam decided to take a stroll outside in the cool night air. Gazing in the moonlight towards the cobblestone road that led ahead to the cliff edge, something strange was happening

The road had extended further out as if the cliff had grown longer. Light shone from cottage windows on each side of its length. Beyond where the clifftop had ended a street now appeared to have materialised.

Surely this was an illusion? He hadn't touched any alcohol that evening. And when he did drink he never consumed enough to imagine things.

Curiosity drove him to approach the amazing vision, walking along the section of road that did exist until he reached the new part that until now had been reclaimed by the sea. In the moonlight he could see a difference in the two cobblestone surfaces. The one that had emerged was not overgrown with grass and weeds.

The strange new street reached out before him. He cautiously stepped forward, testing the ground in case it suddenly disappeared and he'd plunge rapidly to his death far below. But the surface remained firm. The flint stone cottages and road ahead stayed intact.

This was a dream thought Adam. Any second he would wake up in bed. He'd heard the test was to pinch yourself, but he always believed that to be something of a myth. Right now, however, he pinched his forearm - just to be sure.

The street and window lights were still there. As he walked further along the road a cottage door opened and a woman in a long black dress and bonnet came out. She glanced at him briefly, then walked away turning a corner and disappearing from view.

Adam saw other side street turnings as he continued down the road, light shining through the windows of other terraced cottages along their length.

A little further along an oil lamp hanging from a bracket illuminated a sign, The Ship Inn, painted in gold lettering on black hoarding above the door. Light shone through the crown glass windows. Adam could see people moving around inside, but the glass design distorted their images.

He attempted to grasp the situation. By rights, where he stood should have been perhaps a hundred feet or so beyond the cliff edge. But here he was in a place where people obviously lived.

In another test of this strange new reality he decided to enter the inn, pushing open the oak door. Bearded men sitting on stools at wooden tables and a group of four standing at the bar all turned their heads to study this newcomer. Many of them wore navy blue gansey jumpers and thigh length waders.

They reminded Adam of images he'd seen in illustrated history books, depicting coastal village fishermen of the Victorian era. The shadowy scene was lit by oil lamps resting in small wall recesses and on the tables.

He felt eyes following him as he hesitantly approached the bar, unsure whether he was a welcome visitor, arriving beside the group of four men holding pewter tankards of beer.

The heavily built innkeeper wore a dirty white apron covered with brown slop stains. His swept-back, dark greasy hair shone in the lamplight and he eyed Adam suspiciously, the words 'what d'ye want stranger?' needing no voice. He was one of the few clean shaven men on the premises and his face revealed a long, diagonal scar across the right cheek.

"You're the city boy artist come to stay at Mrs Barnaby's cottage," said a man in the gathering beside Adam. He wore a mariner's cap, his face almost lost in a thick ginger beard with deep leathery creases surrounding his smiling eyes.

Adam was confused. How did this man know he was an artist? Well, not an artist in the professional sense. But yes, he dared consider himself such now. And he was puzzled by the man's reference to a Mrs Barnaby, who he seemed to think lived in the cottage.

The innkeeper now looked more at ease with one of his customers recognising the stranger. That being so, Adam was considered acceptable company.

"A pint of beer please," Adam stuttered, still uncertain of the company around in this bizarre setting. The innkeeper lifted a jug of ale from the counter behind him and poured the alcohol into a pewter tankard, placing it on the bar.

"That'll be two pence," he demanded. Adam was amazed, wondering how many years back it would be when a pint of beer cost so little. He reached for his jeans back pocket. But there was no pocket.

At that moment he realised he was no longer wearing his own black jeans and blue T-shirt. Instead, he was clothed in an open-neck high collared white shirt, dark brown waistcoat, beige trousers and brown leather boots.

In a confused state, and with the innkeeper beginning to glare for his money, Adam fumbled over the trousers finding side pockets and some coins inside the right hand one. He grabbed them and placed them on the bar. Strange coins he didn't recognise, but the innkeeper seemed satisfied, taking two of them and leaving the rest, which Adam returned to his pocket.

He had no idea what the coins he retained were worth, or like the clothes, how they had come to him.

"I saw you sketching on the cliff top yesterday while I was making my way to Brampton town," the ginger bearded man standing nearby said to him, slightly raising the peak of his mariner's cap to take a closer look at the artist. The other three men in the gathering concentrated on the newcomer.

Adam felt uncomfortable under their gaze and was puzzled by the man's remark. It was true he'd been sketching on the cliff top, but was unaware of seeing him before. He would certainly have noticed someone wearing that throwback fishermen's clothing, and especially sporting such a generous ginger beard. A woman walking her dog and stopping briefly to see him at work was the only person he'd seen in the remote setting yesterday.

"I'm Abner Harvill," captain of the fishing vessel Maybelle, the man introduced himself. "This scurvy lot of layabouts are my crew," he grinned, sweeping his hand to indicate the men with him.

"That's my son Jasper," he nodded towards a young man with curly ginger hair and a beard of more modest proportions than his father's. "We call him Tadpole, because when he was a little one he fell into a pond teeming with tadpoles. Had to fish him out. Screaming and shouting for his life he was," Abner laughed heartily at the memory. His son grimaced with embarrassment, after suffering the same introduction to newcomers so many times before.

"That's Daniel," Abner nodded towards a wiry looking man in the group with black hair and a bushy beard, who stared at Adam through aggressive narrowed eyes, as if suspecting him of some underhand motive for being there.

"We call him Serious," the captain continued, "because he always looks like a miserable sod." The description raised a smile from the crewman, but Adam sensed anyone other than the captain describing him like that would find themselves a great deal less mobile. Abner obviously commanded his men with a steely iron fist as well as a large body.

"And him there," the captain pointed to the other man in the gathering, "is Longhorn." He began laughing again joined by the other crewmen. "Christ knows why his parents called him that. He's a little short arse." Now they fell about with laughter. The face on the middle-aged man, whose stature was smaller than the rest of them, would have shown glowing red, save for the greying beard covering most of it. He swigged at his beer as if ignoring the remark.

"We call him Charcoal," the captain continued mercilessly, "because he's our galley cook and every bloody thing he turns out is always burnt to a cinder."

The laughter broke into full force again, now even Charcoal joining in, knowing behind Abner's rough exterior they could all depend on his total loyalty and steadfast command at sea, even in the most ferocious of storms.

"And what do they call you?" Adam ventured, wondering immediately if he may have spoken out of turn as the laughing abruptly stopped.

Abner stared at him coldly for a moment before replying.

"To my face they call me Captain, but many other profane names behind my back!" He scowled at his crew, then broke into laughter again, prompting the men to follow. Adam now joined in as Abner slapped him on the back in a friendly gesture, nearly sending him flying with beer slopping over the side of his tankard.

He was warming to the new company and took a swig from the vessel. The beer was flat and sharply bitter, unlike any beer he'd ever tasted. But he refrained from complaining to the innkeeper, who looked as though he would physically eject anyone daring to question the quality of his offerings. Instead he decided to introduce himself to his new companions.

"We couldn't call you by your proper name," the captain announced after the introduction. "No, you're an artist. We'll call you Paintbrush."

His crew nodded agreement and raised their beer mugs, drinking to anoint Adam's new name.

The evening progressed with the crewmen recounting some of their dicier moments in unfriendly seas, and how they'd often outmatched other fishing crews in the village with their catches.

Adam, or Paintbrush, was entranced. Somehow he found himself in another era, listening to and being in the company of people who lived, or had lived in the past. He was unsure which. Their conversation sometimes referred to the new Queen Victoria, who had reigned back in the 19th century.

He was now on his fourth pint of beer. The off-taste had dulled with more drink and he felt amazingly good as well as a little intoxicated. When his fishermen companions asked about his life in the big city of London, they looked puzzled when he referred to the place being full of cars in traffic jams.

"What are cars?" asked Tadpole.

"Motor cars," Adam replied, then realised it would be meaningless to anyone from the century these men appeared to live in.

"Carriages," he explained.

"Well why didn't you say?" asked Charcoal. "Cities are always busy with carriages and carts. My aunt Bessie once went to London. Hated it. Streets full of rubbish. Cramped little places for people to live. No fresh air she told me."

Adam reflected to himself that some areas of the city hadn't changed that much since Charcoal's aunt Bessie went there. He decided to say no more about the modern world. The people here would think him insane talking about things that it seemed hadn't been invented yet.

"Well boys, we've got an early start to catch the tide in the morning," said the captain, slamming his empty beer mug down on the bar. "Time to get some kip."

His crewmen quickly finished their drinks preparing to leave with him.

Adam was starting to feel unsteady on his feet and knew he'd consumed more than enough alcohol.

"We'll be out fishing for the next few days, but we'll probably see you again soon," said Abner, placing his broad hand on Adam's shoulder outside the inn. "Mind yourself drawing on some of those cliffs. Don't get too near the edges 'cause they can give way," he warned.

Adam thanked him for the advice and said he'd return soon. The crewmen made their way down the main road, separating to their homes along side streets. Adam swayed as he walked back up the incline to the cottage. Cloud now obscured the moonlight, but lamps hanging on brackets outside the terraced cottages lining the route gave enough light for him to see his unsteady way home.

Before entering the property, he turned to view the village where he'd spent the evening, expecting to see the lamplights shining. But there was only dark. As moonlight briefly escaped through a gap in the cloud, all he could see was the cliff edge a short distance away. The village was gone.

That was impossible? He couldn't possibly have walked on air? Talked to people? Seen dwellings and the inn where now only the sea existed? The sound of waves breaking on the shore below was audible in the light breeze, confirming the village's absence. Adam groaned, feeling woozy from the ale. That sensation was certainly real enough. He went inside and straight to bed. Images of the fishermen surfaced frequently in his sleep.

CHAPTER 2

NEXT morning Adam awoke wondering if he'd really been in an enchanted village, or was it some kind of hallucination?

He stared out the bedroom window towards the sea. The cliff edge stood as it did before, the overgrown cobblestone road ending at the face.

What had come over him the previous night he wondered while pulling on his T-shirt and jeans? The strange clothes he wore at the inn were nowhere in sight. He checked his money. No alien coins from another era.

Maybe the strain of his former high pressure job was affecting his mind as it began to unwind. The thought frightened him a little. Hallucinating was obviously not good. What might he do if he was losing touch with reality?

Adam forced the doubts to the back of his mind, but couldn't help laughing at the nickname the fishermen in his fantasy had given him. Paintbrush.

Over the next couple of days he spent time sketching seascapes from clifftop vantage points along the coastline, occasional hikers making their way across the remote setting stopping for a chat and to watch him at work.

There was no fridge to preserve food at the cottage and Adam decided that tomorrow he'd go to Brampton the nearest town five miles away to buy fresh provisions.

That evening he worked at the easel in the living room, creating a colourful copy in oils of a coastline sketch. Photography was out. His own memory would add the colour.

It was nearing ten o'clock when he decided to finish what he was doing. As he began to put away the art materials, he felt the strangest sensation of another presence in the room. Looking behind, he saw an elderly woman in a black dress, her grey hair tied in a bun.

"You really should get some rest now," she said to him. "Breakfast will be served at seven thirty, and I don't want you to be late."

Adam's jaw dropped. Who was this woman? He was about to ask when she evaporated. He stood there paintbrush in hand, completely stunned for a while, then went to the kitchen for the bottle of whisky he'd brought along, pouring himself a generous glassful. Maybe his mind was more out of order than he'd realised. He would have to get a grip on these ridiculous phantoms.

That night he laid awake for some time thinking about the strange events he'd experienced since arriving.

In the morning Adam looked out the bedroom window. Curiosity like the last few mornings forced him to see if the village he'd seemingly walked into the other night may have reappeared. Seeing only the clifftop and nothing but sea beyond, he felt reassured that perhaps relaxation was dissolving his imaginings.

For breakfast he ate cereal with milk that was starting to curdle. It was definitely time to get more provisions.

The inland route to Brampton took Adam along narrow hedge bordered lanes, opening occasionally on to cultivated and grazing pastures.

As he entered the town, flint stone cottages lined each side of the high street, many of the ground floors of properties in the central part converted into shops. They weren't exactly shopping emporiums like Adam was accustomed to in London, but that was good he thought. Many appeared more traditional, some reminding him of stores you would have found in smaller towns forty or so years back with hoardings above giving owner names. Cousins the Fruiterer, Ramsay the Grocer, Parson's Ironmongery.

He parked in the high street lay-by and made for the grocery store. The setting inside was small, but the shelves provided enough supplies for his needs.

"A stranger in these parts?" the middle-aged man behind the checkout observed with a welcoming grin as Adam unloaded his purchases from the basket.

"Yes, I've moved into the cottage beside old Coatehaven."

"That used to be Mrs Cartwright's place, God rest her soul," the man recalled, sweeping the goods across the checkout scanner.

"I bought the cottage from her son Danny," Adam replied, loading his purchases into a bag.

"So what brings you here?"

Adam explained his life change plan and art ambition.

"Plenty of beautiful views to paint and draw on the coastline," the assistant commended as he took payment.

Adam prepared to leave when a question came to mind. Perhaps a local could answer.

"I know Mrs Cartwright used to own the cottage I've just bought, but have you ever heard of a Mrs Barnaby?" Adam recalled the name of the woman mentioned as the property owner during his odd encounter the other night, when Coatehaven had seemed to re-appear.

"Barnaby?" the man pondered. "Mrs Barnaby? Can't say as I do," he began, then something seemed to click.

"Ah yes. I remember my grandfather, God rest his soul, telling me when I was a boy about a passed down story of the Barnaby fishing family. They used to live near Coatehaven before it disappeared."

The assistant paused while the memory slowly returned. "Yes, I think the father and two sons perished in a storm at sea, leaving the woman on her own. Reduced to renting a room at her cottage beside the old village to get by." He stopped again. "I'm certain that's what my grandfather told me. Sad business."

Adam began to wonder if he'd made the right choice buying the property. Perhaps it was haunted. Perhaps he hadn't been hallucinating.

******

OVER the next couple of days he set out to draw seascapes again. About a quarter of a mile further along the cliff he found a narrow pathway descending to the shale beach.

The tide was out and he set up the easel to sketch the coastline, with surf softly brushing the shore. This was the peaceful life he'd so wished for.

By mid-afternoon he decided to finish for the day. The sun was becoming increasingly covered by clouds drifting in from the horizon, and a strong breeze had picked up stirring the surf on the incoming tide into higher dives.

Carrying the easel and art case on the steep climb to the top of the cliff was tiring. By the time he'd covered the remaining quarter mile to the cottage, Adam felt in need of a strong cup of tea and a snack.

As he sat in the kitchen drinking the brew, he thought he heard a sound in the hallway. Opening the door, he saw the same elderly woman who'd mysteriously appeared the other night. She was sweeping the hall floor and stopped to look at him.

"Oh, you're back are you? I didn't hear you come in," she said.

Adam froze. Who was this woman?

"The sea's starting to play up rough. Lost my husband and sons William and Jeremiah at sea when the weather started playing up," she told him.

Adam shook himself out of his torpor and was about to speak. Question her. But she evaporated.

He stood in the kitchen doorway for some time, strange thoughts racing through his head. Foremost the recollection of the store man in Brampton telling him about the Barnaby family of years ago. The wife losing her husband and sons at sea. Her living in a cottage beside the old village. Had he just seen the ghost of that woman for a second time?

He looked out the kitchen window, wondering if the weather was 'playing up' as the woman had said. It was now much cloudier, but nothing particularly out of the ordinary. Feeling unsettled he sat down to finish his tea, fearing that perhaps he really was starting to lose touch with reality.

He'd brought along a radio and tuned into a music station. It was the first time he sought entertainment from the outside world since arriving, and soon the sound filling the room settled his nerves.

That evening, after a ready meal dinner he listened to more music in the living room, reviewing the sketches he'd drawn that day, then decided to take a stroll outside in the fresh sea air.

Stepping outside, Adam looked towards the cliff, then stepped back staring in utter amazement. The village had re-appeared. Almost mesmerised he walked towards it, and as he neared, night-time turned to day, the cottages lining the cobblestone high street perfectly visible.

He closed his eyes, trying to blot out what must be a trick of imagination or an hallucination. Slowly he opened them again, expecting the night returned and the village gone. But the light remained as well as the village. The ground beneath supported him the other night when he ventured into the high street, surely it could again. Adam felt himself drawn towards the setting and began approaching.

As he entered in the daylight, he could see shops on the ground floors of many cottages along the street selling clothes, ironmongery, leather goods, animal foodstuffs, candles and lamplights. Women wearing bonnets and long dresses made their way along the road going into the shops or making their way in and out of the narrow side streets.

A group of fishermen in gansey jumpers, black wool trousers and thigh length boots came along the street towards him.

For a moment he wondered if they were the men he'd seen at the inn. But their faces were not the same, and they passed by loudly discussing something about a mast repair.

Adam continued along the road which began to descend into a steep slope. Below he could see a curved bay with a broad seafront wall that had two piers stretching into the waters at each end. Fishing smacks with tall sails were moored alongside, fishermen busily unloading their catches into large wooden crates, then hoisting them on to horse drawn carts ready for transport to local markets.

Seagull cries filled the air as they hovered and circled above the waters, enviously eyeing the fishermen's hauls and ready to swoop at the chance of a quick snatch. Two of them on the seafront squabbled over a fish that had fallen from a cart, viciously pecking at each other for possession.

For a while Adam stood transfixed by the sight. In his own modern world the fishing industry at most coastal towns and villages had virtually disappeared. Here, it seemed, he was witnessing the way it used to happen back in the day of his forefathers.

"Get out the way!" a man shouted loudly from behind, bringing Adam abruptly out of his trance. He swung round. The man held the reins of another horse drawn cart rapidly rattling over the cobblestones towards him. Adam leapt aside, his heart pounding as the cart narrowly missed mowing him down.

"You must be careful along here," a woman's voice from behind made him turn again. She wore a dark blue bustle dress, layered with frills, and light blue ruffled brim bonnet. Adam was immediately captured by the young woman's smile and gleaming eyes. Her nose was slightly upturned, and light brown hair ringlets protruded beneath the rim of the bonnet.

"Yes, I'll be careful," he replied, surprised by her sudden appearance.

"You won't find a lot of gentlemen around here," she said, continuing to smile. "I'm sure artists like yourself live a much more cultured life."

Adam was further surprised. How did she know he was an artist? A self-appointed one at any rate. She anticipated his question.

"It's a small village. Gossip travels quickly. You're staying with Mrs Barnaby I believe?"

Adam nodded. Of course he wasn't staying with a Mrs Barnaby, but it seemed pointless at that moment to dispute her belief.

"So now I shall bid you good-day," the woman smiled at him again, then walked away towards a baker's shop a little further up the incline in the road.

Adam would have liked to spend more time in the company of the woman, but she was gone before he could think of anything else to say. He walked back along the road heading for The Ship Inn, wondering if the fishermen he'd met a few nights before would be there again.

Several fishermen with mugs of beer sat chatting at a table, but there was no sign of his new found companions. The innkeeper had seen Adam enter and presented a slightly less hostile face to him knowing he wasn't a complete stranger.

"A pint of beer?" the man asked, just as Adam was about to turn and leave. He hadn't planned on drinking by himself, but decided to stay for one ale.

At that moment he realised the money he carried was not the currency of this strange world he found himself in, but swiftly became aware his clothing had transformed into the same high collar white shirt, waistcoat and trousers that he'd been wearing the other night at the inn.

For a second he was thrown, trying to grasp the situation, fearing again he was losing his mind. And yet here he was. Everything seemed so real. He reached into his trouser pocket and pulled out unrecognisable coins, placing them on the bar. The innkeeper selected the pennies he needed and handed the pewter mug to Adam.

"Has Captain Abner returned with his crew yet?" he asked the innkeeper.

"No," came the gruff reply, "another crew reported there's a thick mist hanging around further out to sea. Abner's probably anchored down 'til it clears." The innkeeper stared at Adam for a few moments as if thinking this inn is no place for stranger city boys, then turned and entered a door behind the bar, leaving Adam feeling unnerved by the man's obvious disapproval of him.

He decided to quickly finish his drink. The only other people in the room were the fishermen at the nearby table now starting to play cards. All the other inn regulars he surmised were probably at sea or unloading their catches on the pier.

A few minutes later Adam had finished his ale and prepared to leave as the innkeeper returned to the bar. Adam walked to the door and turned to bid him goodnight in a gesture of friendship, even though he didn't expect it to be reciprocated. As he opened his mouth to speak, cold terror shot through him. A skeleton stood behind the bar. Adam gaped speechless. In the same second the skeleton was gone replaced by the innkeeper staring at him.

"Are you well?" the man asked, seeing the horrified expression on his face. Adam stuttered he was okay, though feeling far from it. The innkeeper shook his head wondering why his customer had looked so terrified.

Adam left and made his way back to the cottage convincing himself that he'd had some brief mental aberration. He attempted to put the experience to the back of his mind, but continued to tremble for a while.

As he entered the cottage he became aware of being in his denim shirt and jeans again. Another weird experience of transformation that troubled him, and yet oddly also gave him a thrill. The unique ability of crossing between two different worlds.

Going into the kitchen to make a coffee, his phone on the counter beside the cooking range began ringing. That surprised him as there was barely any signal in the area. He answered.

"Adam?" came the faint sound of a woman's voice. "It's Josie."

"Line's awful. Are you okay?" he asked his wife.

"Yes, I'm fine. Are you settling in at your new cottage?"

"It's amazing. You really must come and see. There's something here I'd love to show you," Adam enthused. For a moment buzzing on the line made the connection sound as if it was cutting out.

"Josie?"

"I'm still here. Better be quick before we lose the signal. I was wondering if we could meet? I want to talk to you about something."

"About what?" Adam sounded intrigued.

"Better if we meet," Josie replied.

"Come down here to the cottage. I can show you around. And take you to a place you just wouldn't believe. Come here tomorrow."

"It's a long drive from where I am, and was wondering if we could meet up somewhere halfway? Your place in London?" she asked. Josie lived with their teenage children and her partner David on the opposing western coastline to Adam's cottage in the east, around 200 miles apart.

"But there's something really amazing happening here. I'd really like you to come quickly. It might disappear for good for all I know." Adam insisted.

"What is it?" she asked.

"You have to see it for yourself," Adam replied cryptically. "Stay for the night. Use my bed."

Josie was reluctant to make the long drive so soon. It was Thursday and she was working next day. She also had some weekend plans with the family. A shorter journey wouldn't disrupt them. And she certainly hadn't planned to stay overnight at Adam's cottage. This was typical of Adam's impulsive nature when he grasped a sudden idea. Often his ambitious trait when they were together had been admirable, but sometimes it also made her mad.

However, it was a particularly sensitive matter she wanted to talk about, and was coming to the conclusion she'd have to agree to his request. But it would have to be Saturday.

Her partner David was a good man. He'd be annoyed at the change in their weekend plans, but understood why she needed to see him. The youngsters Liam and Olivia would be disappointed. They'd been looking forward to a trip out.

As Adam waited in the moments Josie was making her decision, the kitchen door opened and an elderly woman entered. It was the same woman who'd appeared before, and he was now rapidly coming to the realisation of it being Mrs Barnaby the people in Coatehaven had referred to.

"Oh, you're back are you?" she said, staring at him. Then dissolved into the air.

"Adam, are you still there?" Josie's voice came faintly over the phone. In the distraction he hadn't heard her replying.

"Yes I'm here. Mrs Barnaby just came in."

"Mrs who?"

"Oh nothing." Adam surprised himself by almost believing for a moment that he was renting the cottage from the phantom.

"I'll be there, but it'll have to be Saturday, about midday," Josie told him.

"Wonderful. You won't regret it." His last words were lost. Either the signal was gone or Josie had hung up. Then Adam noticed his phone battery was nearly flat. No electricity in the place to recharge it. Never mind, he could charge it on a run in the Transit sometime soon.

******

THE following morning he set off to draw more clifftop sketches of the coastline, including a high point view overlooking Coatehaven, which continued to remain visible to him.

Returning early evening when the warm air of the day was rapidly cooling, he washed and made his way to the kitchen to prepare a meal.

"I've made you a beef stew for supper," said Mrs Barnaby, turning her head towards him as she stirred the pot on the range with a wooden spoon.

Adam halted in the doorway, staring in amazement.

"I expect you're hungry," the woman continued, standing there in a long black dress and white apron. She picked up a ladle and scooped stew into a china bowl. "Now sit yourself in the front room and I'll bring it to you."

Adam's mind was reeling, struggling to know whether this was a fantasy or really happening. The aroma of the stew was appetising. Something made him feel inclined to obey Mrs Barnaby's request. He went into the living room, which now seemed strangely different, with lace curtains at the windows looking towards the village at the front and a paved garden at the back. The decaying wooden fence wasn't there. Instead a low hedgerow with a field visible behind.

The light pinewood table and chairs that had been left by the previous owner's son were gone, replaced by a different darker table and high backed chairs. The fireplace that had been covered over was now open with a flickering log fire. Something bizarre was happening, but Adam felt cosy, the atmosphere inviting and a prepared meal on the way.

"The beef for the stew is fresh from the market, and tomorrow you can have herrings cooked fresh from the day's catch," Mrs Barnaby told Adam as she entered and placed the bowl on the table for him.

He picked up the spoon beside it and scooped a mouthful of broth. It was truly delicious. This was as real as reality could feel he thought, spooning up more and enjoying the crackling warmth of the fire.

He'd planned to go into Coatehaven that night to see if Captain Abner and his crew had returned from their fishing trip. But he felt tired, deciding instead to go to his room and look over some of the sketches.

Before retiring to bed he glanced into the night from his bedroom window. The lamps in the village cottages along the high street glittered in the moonlight. Adam felt the sense of being in a place where he belonged. Everything before now had been leading towards this moment.

Then for a second a wave of doubt struck. A voice inside urging him to row back. The image of the man in the smock and bucket hat came to him. But the sensation lasted only briefly. No, this is where he belonged.

CHAPTER 3

JOSIE arrived at the cottage just after noon on Saturday, parking her blue Ford MPV on the gravelled frontage. Adam came to the door and greeted her with a hug. It had been nearly a year since they'd last met.

Her rosy round face and smiling hazel eyes stirred the enduring affection he still held for her. The last time they'd seen each other, long auburn hair had trailed over her shoulders. Now it was cropped back nestling round her neck. She was smartly dressed in a white open neck shirt and dark trouser suit.

"You didn't have to dress so formally to visit me," Adam joked as they entered the cottage.

"I had a meeting early this morning with someone who wants to invest in my beauty salon business. Possibly going to expand it," Josie explained. "I didn't dress up just to see you," she laughed.

"No standing on ceremony with me," he smiled. "Come on, let's make you a coffee." They went into the kitchen.

Josie studied the setting with a quizzical gaze.

"This is a bit of a come down from your high flying executive life. The place needs a major upgrade," she observed.

"A work that will eventually be in progress," said Adam, placing the whistle kettle on the range hot plate. "I love it. Never been so happy for many a year as being here," he reached up for two mugs on a shelf. "How are our lovely children?"

"Doing well at school, though Liam gets too many detentions for messing about in class. Olivia is showing great talent playing in the netball team," Josie told him.

"She's always been good at sport, and as for Liam," Adam paused, "tell me what boys don't get detentions for messing about?" They both smiled.

"And what is it you want to talk about?" he enquired, spooning coffee powder into the mugs.

Josie faltered, looking slightly at ease in replying.

"Nothing wrong is there?" Adam asked, noticing her reluctance.

Steam began spewing from the spout of the kettle setting off a shrill whistle. Adam used a tea towel to grip the hot handle and poured the water into the mugs.

"No milk or sugar if I remember," he glanced at her. She shook her head.

"Come into the living room and we'll talk." He led her into the room carrying the coffee.

"What's the problem?" Adam coaxed again as they sat at the table.

"I've come to ask if you would grant me a divorce," Josie decided to get straight to the point.

Adam remained silent for a moment as her request sank in. They'd been separated for some time and he'd become used to continuing their lives apart without being divorced. He'd never met another woman he wanted to spend the rest of his days with, so the business of divorcing hadn't entered his thoughts.

"You want to marry David, I presume?" said Adam, returning from his thoughts. Josie nodded.

Adam had met David a couple times when visiting the children to take them on an outing. A good looking man about the same age, they both got on reasonably well together, given that Adam had accepted his close relationship with Josie was over. He'd even come to accept the children being brought up in the partnership. David had proved to be a caring man.

But divorce? It would represent the final severance.

Josie could read the turmoil in Adam's mind.

"Nothing else will change," she assured him. "Everything will go on as it was. You'll always be free to visit the children. It's just I want to make things right for David. He wants to marry me. Make the relationship proper. Call us old fashioned if you like." Josie smiled pleadingly. "It would be good if it could be done cleanly with agreement. No disputing."

Adam remained silent again for a while before coming to a decision.

"Well yes, I'll give you a divorce on one condition," he replied.

Josie's eyes narrowed wondering what condition. Would it be reasonable?

"On condition you spend the night here. I want to show you the most incredible place. A village that disappeared into the sea many years ago. It has come back." Adam expected her to share wonder at his revelation. But Josie appeared totally perplexed. What joke was this he had in mind?

"You might have seen the place as you arrived," Adam continued enthusiastically. "Come on, I'll show you at the front door," he stood up and she followed.

"There you are," he opened the door and pointed ahead. The village's terraced cottages were visible to him. Josie stared, but could see nothing except the cliff edge and sea beyond.

"Stop playing the fool, I can't see any village," she laughed.

"Can't you?" Adam turned to her completely mystified. For a brief second he began to wonder if he was losing his mind. He turned back to look again at the village. Now all he could see was the cliff end. The place had disappeared.

"Are you alright?" Josie looked concerned.

"It was there. I've visited it. Spoken to people who live there," Adam insisted.

Now it was Josie who was beginning to wonder if he'd lost his mind.

"I'll prove it to you. I'm certain you'll be able to see the place tonight. You can join me in visiting it." Adam wouldn't let go of believing the village existed.

Josie had already decided she would agree to Adam's request to stay the night, but was now having second thoughts. He was exhibiting odd behaviour and didn't seem to be joking as Josie first thought. Perhaps something she was not aware of had tipped his mind. She hadn't seen him in a year. Maybe he was having some sort of breakdown and that's why he chose to get away from it all.

"I know I said I'd stay, but in all honesty I'd rather drive back home tonight if you don't mind. Stay another time soon," she began her excuse to leave. "I'd planned to go out with David and the children to the zoo tomorrow."

"The condition for the divorce is you stay for one night. It's not a lot to ask," Adam insisted. "You can surely put up with slumming it for one night."

Josie felt something had changed in him. She couldn't nail it down, just something different. However, she wanted an uncomplicated divorce and an overnight stay would be a small price to pay.

During the afternoon Adam showed her some of his drawings and paintings of seascapes, and Josie expressed genuine admiration for his artistic talent. He'd obviously improved technique in the years they'd been apart.

It was when he showed her the sketch he'd drawn of Coatehaven from the clifftop that she began to wonder about him again.

Adam insisted it was the village that she'd apparently been unable to see. It was definitely a village layout, and looked as though it was from a past era, but he could have drawn it from an old sketch or painting of a village she thought. Not wishing to get into an argument and jeopardise the point of her visit, Josie just accepted what he wanted her to believe.

After another coffee, they set off for a walk along the clifftops nearby.

Her misgivings about staying for the night softened as she enjoyed the fresh air and beautiful coastline views, the sea rippling a deep blue under the cloudless sky. They chatted about earlier times together, remembering amusing incidents and places they'd visited.

As they walked, Josie couldn't help noticing him occasionally glancing back towards the cliff edge that fronted the cottage.

"What are you looking at?" she eventually asked.

"It was definitely there," Adam replied. "I've visited it. Spoken to the inhabitants. The fishermen who live there. They've nicknamed me Paintbrush."

"*What* was there?"

"I've told you. The village of Coatehaven. Just because we can't see it right now, doesn't mean it isn't there." Adam sounded frustrated the place was no longer visible, leaving him unable to prove the spectacle.

Doubts began to surface in Josie's mind again. For a short time in their stroll she had begun to relax remembering happier past times. She had also wondered if perhaps his references to seeing a lost village re-appearing from the sea was a fiction he'd made up, and would eventually admit he was just playing a hoax on her. 'I really had you wondering, didn't I?" she was hoping he would come clean. Now she had misgivings again about staying the night. But she'd have to stick to the agreement.

They returned to the cottage as the sun began setting, blending a purple and red haze across the horizon.

Adam prepared a meal of fresh plaice and vegetables that he'd bought that morning in Brampton. Josie was impressed by his culinary skill, especially cooking on an old range instead of a modern oven.

"Living on my own for so long has taught me to be adaptable," he said, as they sat at the living room table. He topped up their glasses of wine. Adam felt sad that his marital bond with Josie would soon be broken. It had continued to be a link between them even though they'd been apart for some time. But it would be selfish to obstruct the future of a woman he had dearly loved. And still did in many ways. The time had come to finally let go.

They finished the meal and spent more time chatting over another glass of wine, with LED lamps now lighting the downstairs setting. Then they washed the plates and saucepans in the deeply marked and chipped ceramic kitchen sink. It reminded them of the flat they'd moved into soon after marrying.

"And now I'm going to show you the village," he announced.

The old self Adam that Josie began warming to during the meal quickly dissolved. He'd returned to his obsession about some imaginary village.

He took hold of a lamp and led her to the front door. Opening it he pointed towards the cliff, where he saw cottage lights shining in the darkness. Josie looked. All she could see was the darker shade of the cliff edge against starlight on the sea's horizon.

"What village?" she asked, still hoping Adam was continuing with a practical joke.

"Coatehaven. Can't you see it? The place has returned." Adam sounded frustrated.

"No."

"Come with me." He held out the lamp and began walking towards the cliff. Josie reluctantly followed, expecting Adam would now have to admit it was a hoax. But he continued, drawing dangerously close to the edge.

"Stop!" Josie screamed. The terror in her voice made him halt abruptly.

"What's wrong?" he swung round.

"For God's sake you're about to fall over. This joke has gone far enough."

"It's no joke. I'm about to enter the village. I can't understand why you aren't able to see it." Adam was genuinely perplexed.

"There is no bloody village. Now whether this is a joke or not, your fooling around will get you killed," Josie was furious as well as frightened of what might happen. "If you keep doing this I'm getting in the car right now and driving home."

Adam was deeply disappointed she couldn't see Coatehaven. But he didn't want her to leave. He'd been enjoying her company and just wanted to hold the moment for a little longer before their knot was finally severed.

"Okay, we'll go back. I didn't mean to upset you," he relented. Josie breathed a sigh of relief.

"I don't want you playing any more practical jokes on me," she said as they returned inside the cottage. Adam wanted to argue the point that it wasn't a joke, but was worried it would cause her to leave if he persisted and kept quiet.

"I can't offer you any TV programmes to watch and there's no Wi-Fi either, though I do have a pack of cards," he changed the subject. Josie remembered days when they'd sometimes played cards together in the evenings. She settled with him at the kitchen table beside the warmth of the range, sipping wine and playing whist.

At ten o'clock they decided to turn in for the night. Adam showed Josie to his bedroom. The sleeping bag on the mattress didn't exactly match the high standards of The Ritz she observed sarcastically, but it would do for one night.

"Bathroom's just along the landing. I'll be kipping in the living room. If there's anything you need let me know," he told her. "Tomorrow morning my landlady Mrs Barnaby will be making breakfast for us. She serves it at seven thirty."

Josie stared at him bewildered. Mrs Barnaby? His landlady? Was this some new practical joke?

Adam held a straight face. It appeared he really meant it. She was about to question him further about Mrs Barnaby when he wished her goodnight and left the room.

She laid awake feeling extremely uncomfortable in the sleeping bag. But her mind was even more disquieted. Adam seemed to be switching strangely in behaviour. Totally rational for a while, then manifesting very odd beliefs. He wasn't playing jokes. She really was becoming convinced he had some sort of mental disorder.

Perhaps his life as a high-powered sales executive had damaged his psyche? Maybe he needed psychiatric help? She had an uneasy night both physically and mentally, and looked forward to returning home.

Catching very little of what could be called proper sleep, Josie rose at seven next morning and went downstairs to make a coffee. She heard snoring coming from the living room and looked in to see Adam curled up asleep on the floor wearing his jeans and T-shirt.

In the kitchen the range plate was still hot enough to boil the kettle, and she refilled the grate with some logs from a pile by the side to keep the fire burning.

Then she remembered Adam saying that a Mrs Barnaby would be preparing breakfast. Josie wondered if some local woman she hadn't yet met would be calling. Adam had strangely referred to her as his landlady, but she apparently didn't live in the cottage. Anyway, as far as she knew, he'd bought the property, so why would he be renting from someone?

She made two mugs of coffee and was about to call Adam when he entered the kitchen looking unshaven and his clothes crumpled from sleeping on the floor.

"Morning. Did you sleep well?" he greeted.

"Not the most comfortable night," Josie expressed her honest opinion.

"That'll all be fixed when I order some proper furniture and refurbish the place," he replied, taking the coffee Josie held out for him.

"Where's this Mrs Barnaby who's meant to be making breakfast?" she asked.

"Did I say that?" Adam appeared puzzled. "Don't remember." He took a sip of coffee. "I might have been getting confused. The fishermen I met in the village said I was staying with her. Don't know why they think that."

Now it was Josie who looked puzzled.

"You mean the imaginary village you keep going on about. I've told you to stop playing this silly hoax."

"It's no hoax, it's really there," Adam continued to insist.

Josie had planned to stay for breakfast, but had now taken enough of her husband's strange behaviour. He really seemed to believe in some sort of phantoms.

"I'm going now," she told him, taking a drink of coffee before preparing to leave.

"Can't you stay a bit longer. I'll cook you something to eat before you go," Adam pleaded.

"No, I'll stop off somewhere on the way back. I've kept my part of the bargain and stayed overnight, I expect you to keep yours."

Adam looked disappointed, but nodded in accepting she'd done as asked. Josie collected her belongings and made her way to the car.

"Next time you come, bring the children along," said Adam as she climbed into the vehicle. "They'll love it here by the sea."

"Yes, I'll be in touch to sort something out," she promised, though uncertain as to whether they should see their father behaving so oddly.

She drove away and Adam returned inside, sad at Josie's sudden parting, but looking forward to meeting his fishermen friends at the inn that evening. They would probably be back from their fishing expedition by now. He was unaware that the easygoing image he'd built of them in his mind, would soon be shattered.

CHAPTER 4

AFTER Josie's departure, Adam hiked to locations along the clifftops again. This time he took his easel and art case to paint seascapes and bay settings in oils instead of sketching.

Early evening he heated a tinned steak pie for dinner, then set off for the inn at Coatehaven. It remained a mystery to him that Josie had been unable to see the village.

The lamplights shining from the cottage windows and hanging from door-side brackets lit his way along the cobblestone road, as he headed for the alehouse.

"It's Paintbrush," Abner's voice boomed as Adam entered. The captain and his crew were gathered at the bar.

"A beer for our resident artist," he ordered the landlord. The welcome made Adam feel good. He was becoming accepted in the community.

As the innkeeper placed the ale on the counter, a brief wave of fear coursed through Adam, remembering the man's skeletal frame appearing when he was last there. Fortunately no such image re-appeared and he relaxed.

"Been living the easy life painting pictures, while me and the lads have been working like dogs at sea earning a bloody pittance?" the captain goaded him with a crafty smile. Adam took the remark in good humour, but couldn't deny life was greatly more comfortable for him than for the present company.

"That bloody mist," said the captain's crewmate Serious, recalling their encounter at sea. "Thought we'd be stuck for days."

"Don't be so bloody miserable," Abner barked back. "The way you kept moaning you'd think we were doomed. Wasn't as bad as when we were caught in that storm last year, and the vessel near shook itself to pieces."

The captain's son, Tadpole, and Charcoal the cook nodded vigorously recalling the occasion.

Adam listened spellbound as they related tales of dangerous encounters at sea, each of them knowing that life could be wiped away in the sudden sweep of a tempest. And yet they remained undaunted.

As the evening drew on, and three mugs of beer later, Adam said he'd like to make some sketches and paintings of them.

"You can do mine, but I wouldn't bother with the rest of these ugly bastards," the captain boomed, his crew joining in hearty laughter.

The merriment abruptly stopped as three redcoat soldiers burst through the inn door, raising muskets at them and staring fiercely under their tricorner hats.

"Remain where you are!" commanded the redcoat in the centre. "We have reason to suspect you've been importing contraband into the country against government regulations. We are here to search the premises."

Captain Abner and his crew stood absolutely still. Men at the tables ceased their conversations, all eyes focussed on the soldiers. Adam felt his knees begin to tremble uncontrollably. His mind started to wander through two streams of reality. He wasn't really here. This was an other world fantasy. But his fear was real enough. He swayed a little as both psyches wrestled with each other.

"Don't move!" a redcoat shouted, seeing Adam swaying. The soldier pointed the musket directly at him.

Silence descended for a few seconds. Then a group of fishermen who'd been in a corner out of the soldiers' sight suddenly leapt out at them. A musket shot rang out. The metal shot flew into the ceiling as the soldier was pulled to the ground. The other two soldiers were unable to fire as more attackers wrenched away their weapons.

Captain Abner and his crew joined in the fight, deftly producing fish gutting knives sheathed in their back pockets. Adam watched in horror as they viciously plunged the blades into the redcoats, blood spilling out across the flagstone floor.

Abner was on his knees, drawing a blood soaked knife from the body of his victim. He turned to see Adam staring in disbelief.

"Get out! It's nothing to do with you. And keep your bloody mouth shut!"

Adam needed no second prompting. He fled from the chaos, only to be confronted outside by four more redcoats approaching with muskets raised.

"Get out bastards!" Shouting came from a growing crowd of villagers further down the street. Distracted, the soldiers turned their guns away from Adam, moving forward to fend off the increasing numbers of protesters.

"Quick! This way."

Adam heard a woman's voice calling to him from his left. He turned and saw her beckoning to him. He followed in preference to being filled with musket shot. The woman led him down several side streets and then along a narrow alleyway, arriving at the back door of a terraced cottage. She opened it.

"Quick, inside!"

Adam entered a hallway lit by an oil lamp on the side table. She led him into a small living room, a wood mantelpiece over the fireplace, table and chairs, and a cat nestled on an armchair. Two lamps resting at each end of a long shelf lit the room.

"There'll be havoc in the village for a while," the woman said, removing her headscarf.

In the lamplight Adam could now see her face. It only took a moment for him to realise she was the woman who'd spoken to him near the seafront the other day.

"Thank you for rescuing me," said Adam. "I thought I was going to be shot. What the hell is going on?"

The woman was about to reply when shouting and the sound of musket fire echoed down the hallway through the room's open door. She left and Adam followed as she made her way along another passage. It opened into a footwear shop at the front of the premises, boots and shoes displayed on shelves around the room. A broad window overlooked the village high street.

They could see a mob of men outside overpowering the redcoats, beating them to the ground in a frenzied attack.

"What the hell is going on?" Adam repeated.

"Help me," the woman ignored his question, she was opening two wide fronted cupboard doors at the side of the shop and starting to shift a heavy wooden shutter.

"It's too dangerous to fit an outer one, but we can fix this one inside to limit any damage," she said. Adam quickly rushed to assist her carrying it. They took each end, placing the shutter on a narrow shelf just below the window. As Adam held it in position, she removed a long plank from the cupboard, securing it across the board in brackets each side of the frontage.

The obstruction dulled the sound of the commotion outside and saved them from seeing the violent mayhem.

"What is going on?" Adam repeated yet again.

"There's more going on in the village than just fishing," she said. "Come into the kitchen and I'll make some tea."

Adam was amazed at how coolly the woman was taking the situation. She could see the concern on his face.

"Don't worry. The villagers have no axe to grind with us. A broken shop window is the worst we might suffer."

He followed her into the kitchen, which reminded him of his own at the cottage, a cooking range with a work counter beside it as well as a small table and chairs. However, he didn't have a framed engraving of a young Queen Victoria hanging on the wall. The woman noticed Adam studying it.

"That's my father's," she explained. "He thinks the young Queen's reign is the start of a great era."

Her words confirmed to Adam that he was in a world that existed a long time ago. Queen Victoria's reign started in 1837. It was a world that Adam was finding himself more and more drawn towards. Except the muffled sound of the mob outside echoing down the hallway reminded him that it also held danger. The romantic image he'd built of Captain Abner and his crew had been shattered. Until now he had only seen their friendly side.

"I'm Charlotte Robson," the woman introduced herself, pulling a chair from the table. "Sit down while I make the tea." She turned back to the range and continued talking.

"I understand you've been given the name Paintbrush by some of the locals. Do you want me to call you that, or by some other?"

Adam told the woman his real name, offering her a choice.

"Your real name is good for me," she replied, pouring hot water from the kettle into a brown teapot on the counter beside the range then placing it on the table.

"You want to know what's going on," she said, taking cups and saucers from a cupboard and setting them near the teapot.

"It seemed such a peaceful place," Adam sounded saddened by the violent disruption that had gripped the village. Charlotte sat on a chair beside him.

"It is most of the time," she explained, "but the fishermen get involved with things that earn them far more money than the meagre living to be made from fishing alone."

Adam looked mystified.

"Smuggling," she said, lifting the teapot and pouring the liquid through a strainer into the cups, then adding milk from a jug. "Sugar?" she asked, lifting a bowl. Adam shook his head.

"Not all fishing trips they make are for catching fish. They sometimes cross the North Sea to the nearby continent to pick up spirits, brandy, rum, liqueurs, to sell it on to inns across our region."

Now Adam understood the soldiers' accusation of importing contraband. The fishermen were evading paying tax on the alcohol.

"Someone's informed the authorities," Adam made the obvious guess.

"Someone certainly has," Charlotte replied. "We've had raids from the constabulary before. But this time the authorities have sent in soldiers. It seems they're getting serious. I can only think the landlord of The Ship Inn, who's the main contact for distribution, has a big supply stored in his cellar at present." She paused, taking a sip of her tea.

The sound of the mob outside was beginning to die down.

"But they're murdering the soldiers. They'll make it ten times worse for themselves," Adam couldn't see the sense in it.

"What soldiers?" she asked enigmatically.

"The ones out there," he was mystified by her question.

"Well a fishing vessel can carry bodies as well as fish. Tied to heavy weights they can sink to the sea floor." Charlotte placed her cup back in the saucer.

Adam was shocked by the strategy of cold-blooded murder.

"But surely they'll send more soldiers when their comrades don't return," Adam pursued the logic.

"They won't find them here. It was only a small number they sent. They'll be suspicious, but there won't be anything to show they ever arrived. And there are many thieves and vagabonds in the woods and countryside on the way from the soldiers' base twenty miles away. Could be they were set upon. Who knows?"

Adam couldn't believe the heartlessness of her words. She saw it.

"Well if you'd like to go and inform the authorities of what happened, you are free to do so. But I wouldn't return to this place." She took another sip of tea. "I live here with my father. This is our entire life. We don't have your freedom. Unless we want a boat trip to the bottom of the sea."

Adam now understood exactly the position Charlotte found herself in.

She stood up. The sound of the mob outside was diminishing. Adam followed as she made her way back into the shop.

"It's over," she said, indicating for him to help her remove the protective wood shutter. They looked out the window.

In the shadowy lamplight of the cottages, they could see a group of men loading soldiers bodies on to a horse drawn cart. Shortly it set off towards the bay. Adam could hardly believe he was witnessing this murderous disposal. His conception of the village was now completely transformed. Beneath the veneer of a seemingly peaceful community lay an underbelly of cut throat villainy.

"Give it a little longer and you'll be safe to go," she said. "Come and finish your tea." They returned to the kitchen table.

"You come from London," Charlotte changed the subject. "I've never been there. Lived here all my life. My father is in London on business. Goes there from time to time. He says there are too many carriages and busy highways. People rushing everywhere."

Other than its constant rush, Adam was certain she wasn't referring to the London era he knew. His strange transformation in clothing and money when he entered the village did not arouse suspicion he was from another time. If he told her that, she would think him insane. He'd give a brief description of himself and hopefully avoid any references to modern life.

"I worked in the City as an investment broker dealing in commodities. I've made enough money to pursue my life's interest in painting and drawing, so I'm taking time out to do that while staying at Mrs Barnaby's."

For a second Adam's mind struggled. In that moment he really believed he'd been an investment broker and was staying at Mrs Barnaby's. The switch from present to past was starting to confuse him.

"I see you own a footwear shop," he said, guiding the conversation away from himself and taking a drink of tea.

"It's my father's business. He makes boots and shoes in the workshop at the back. I serve the customers," Charlotte explained. "But it isn't interesting like painting and drawing. I'd love to be able to do that."

"It isn't difficult," Adam encouraged. "I'll show you how if you like."

"Would you?" Charlotte's eyes beamed.

"Of course. Join me when I'm sketching on the clifftops. I'll show you some of the techniques. Tomorrow if you like?"

"Can't tomorrow, but the day after," said Charlotte.

"Perfect." Adam was delighted at the thought of having someone interested in art, as well as such attractive company. "I'll call for you in the morning, day after tomorrow."

Charlotte agreed, then got up from the chair.

"I think you'll be safe to go now," she said. "Let's check."

Adam followed her as she made her way back to the shop and peered out the window. The street was empty. The dark deeds of the night had disappeared from view.

Charlotte opened the front door. As Adam stepped outside a flash of lightning lit the street, swiftly followed by a loud crash of thunder. Adam flinched for a second taken by surprise. He was certain he felt the ground shake underfoot a little.

"Something wrong?" asked Charlotte.

"That thunder and lightning made me jump. I must be on edge after the fighting."

"What thunder and lightning?" Charlotte looked puzzled.

"Didn't you see and hear it? The ground shook a bit." Now Adam was puzzled.

"No," she replied, shaking her head.

Adam felt certain he hadn't imagined it. But then mysterious events seemed to have entered his life. He was finding it harder to distinguish between the two states of past and present.

"Doesn't matter," he said, seeing her mystified expression. "The day after tomorrow I'll call for you."

They wished each other goodnight and he set off back to the cottage. The atmosphere of the uncannily quiet and deserted high street made him feel slightly spooked, the setting now giving no hint of the riotous behaviour just less than an hour before.

******

MRS Barnaby appeared from the kitchen door as Adam entered the cottage. She wore an olive green apron over her long black dress.

"Oh, I'm so glad you're safe," she greeted him, her face filled with relief. "I was worried sick you might have come to grief in all that commotion with the soldiers. Come on, have some warming beef broth before you go to bed." She turned and re-entered the kitchen.

An oil lamp on a stand lit the hall as Adam approached. Now his mind was totally thrown. He wasn't staying with Mrs Barnaby. It was his cottage. She didn't live here. And yet the aroma of the broth wafting from the kitchen was tantalising. He was hungry. Why not?

Another lamp burned on the kitchen table.

"Sit down," the elderly woman nodded towards a chair at the table, then began ladling the broth from a pot on the range into a white china bowl, placing it in front of him.

The broth tasted delicious and Mrs Barnaby smiled with satisfaction when he complimented her cooking. As he spooned the savoury liquid, he glanced at his phone resting nearby on the table. For a moment the black rectangular object with a dark screen puzzled him. Then he remembered and reached to pick it up.

The screen lit as he pressed the side button and showed the battery was low.

"Must recharge it with a drive to town tomorrow," he thought.

"What's the matter?" Mrs Barnaby had turned from the range to ask if Adam wanted more broth and saw him staring at the open palm of his hand.

"Just checking my phone," he replied.

"Your what?" the woman appeared mystified.

"My phone," Adam held it out to give her a better view.

The woman grew more mystified as Adam began to realise it was probably invisible to her. It dawned on him that in this past world that entwined him, people would not be able to see devices that hadn't yet been invented. His mind began to spin again, trying to fathom in which reality it existed, making him a little giddy. He felt a hand on his shoulder.

"You need to get some rest," Mrs Barnaby's voice broke into his clouded brain. "It must have been terrifying for you in the village tonight with those soldiers raiding the place," her words comforted him like a loving grandmother.

She poured him a glass of water from a jug on the counter and handed it to him. He drank, easing the dryness in his throat brought on by the giddiness.

"It *was* terrifying," said Adam, resting back in the chair. Reaction to the horror of the carnage was now starting to surface, delayed only to maintain sanity through the blood soaked killings he'd witnessed at the inn.

Mrs Barnaby pulled out another chair from the table and sat down beside him. He described what he'd witnessed as the villagers attacked, and how Charlotte had saved him.

"Yes I know Charlotte Robson," she said, "a good woman who works for her father Jack at the footwear shop."

When Adam had finished his account, Mrs Barnaby remained silent for a moment before speaking.

"You must never say a word to anyone outside the village what you witnessed tonight," she advised him. "The villagers take very seriously anyone who betrays their secret activities, and you could end up at the bottom of the sea lashed to a heavy weight."

The warning of retribution was similar to Charlotte's portrayal of a traitor's fate, but seemed all the more shocking directed at him, especially from a woman who otherwise appeared so kind and grandmotherly.

"The people here have been nothing but good to me," he replied. "I would never betray them."

"I'm sure you can be trusted," Mrs Barnaby's serious face turned briefly to a smile. Then it fell as another thought surfaced.

"Heaven knows, the fishermen and their families struggle enough to survive on very small incomes, while the government robs them in taxes." The woman sounded bitter. "My husband, Daniel, and sons William and Jeremiah sometimes needed to smuggle spirits for us to survive. The fish catch wasn't always enough. Bad weather could stand them down for days, a week or more even in the winter months," she gazed wistfully, memory welling.

"When they drowned in a storm at sea, it was only the goodwill of the villagers that sustained me through that terrible time. And they still help me to this day."

Adam saw small tear droplets forming in the eye corners of her wrinkled face. She raised a hand to wipe them away.

"Silly me," she said, "fancy me starting to cry at my age."

Adam instinctively wanted to put a comforting arm around her shoulders, but she stood up resuming control of her emotion.

"Right, finish your broth and get yourself to bed," Mrs Barnaby insisted. The contents were now lukewarm, but Adam obeyed not wishing to offend her. She returned to the range and shielding her hand with a cloth, gripped the handle of the cooking vessel to place it on the counter beside.

"Now I'm off to bed," she said, untying the apron around her dress and resting it over the back of the chair she'd been sitting on. "You'll do as well to do the same," she advised Adam again. "Breakfast is at seven thirty." Mrs Barnaby left the kitchen while Adam finished the broth.

Preparing to leave, he stood up looking for the sink to rinse the bowl and spoon. There wasn't one. He placed it on the counter beside the broth pot. His mind was confused. He couldn't remember if there had been a sink in the room.

At the kitchen door he turned to glance back. The broth pot along with the bowl and spoon had disappeared. And the sink under the window had reappeared. What was happening? Had he just imagined Mrs Barnaby? The meal? He felt exhausted, desperately in need of sleep.

Upstairs the bedroom was lit by an oil lamp on an oak dresser. His basic sleeping bag arrangement had disappeared, replaced by a bed with sheets and two brown blankets. He approached it, mystified by the appearance, but enticed by an arrangement looking much cosier than his sleeping bag on a thin mattress. He examined the bed. The wool mattress replacement was much more substantial and comfortable to rest on. He undressed and climbed in, soon descending into a deep sleep.

CHAPTER 5

ADAM woke feeling refreshed. Sunlight streamed through the uncurtained window, making even the dark green, peeling paintwork on the walls appear slightly less unsightly. For a second or so he wondered where he was. Then he recalled the grisly events of yesterday.

But something in the room had changed. Last night he climbed into a cosy bed. Now he became aware of being in his sleeping bag on the original bedstead. Mrs Barnaby? The broth she'd given him last night? Was that real?

There had been a dresser with an oil lamp on it. Both had gone. His LED lamp rested on the wooden floorboards nearby, his watch beside. He looked at it. The time was just after eight. Mrs Barnaby, if she existed, had told him breakfast was at seven thirty.

Quickly he dressed and went down to the kitchen. It was deserted. No sign of the woman, and the cooking range had gone cold after not being refuelled.

Mrs Barnaby had seemed so real. Now he began to wonder if he'd imagined the village and the soldiers' raid? Charlotte? Was he really losing his mind? He began to panic, rushing outside to see if the village was still there.

He looked towards the coastline. The cobblestone road stretched out. Adam could see the cottages lining its length as the highway gradually dipped out of sight to the seafront below.

His emotions rocked. Part of him was happy that Coate-haven had not disappeared. He was growing yet more attached to the people living there. A bond growing stronger. And yet deep in his mind something troubled him. A sense of losing touch with reality.

However, the doubt soon evaporated. The place must be real. Surely you couldn't interact with ghosts? No, he was able to tune into another world, he reasoned, a dimension that others could not see. It was a special gift. That would be the explanation.

Unable to heat water on the range to make tea or coffee, and feeling like eating a proper cooked breakfast, Adam decided to drive into Brampton to find a cafe. He'd seen a tea room in Coatehaven, but the food was limited to breads and cakes. Anyway, the outing would make a change he thought.

The traffic and bustle of people in the town high street contrasted starkly to the quieter pastures of coastline near his cottage. He parked the van in a bay beside a row of shops close to a cafe called Tasty Bites, which is exactly what he wanted right now.

Walking the short distance towards the cafe entrance, he suddenly realised he'd left his wallet in the vehicle. Turning back, the high street had entirely changed.

Where Adam's van was parked now stood a horse and cart, the animal tethered to a wooden railing. More horse drawn carts scurried up and down the dirt track road. On arriving he'd seen a pharmacy and mini-mart on the other side of the street, but now there was a store with a hoarding displaying John Edwards - Corn Merchant. Brown hessian sacks of seed and animal foodstuffs were stacked on a raised wooden entrance porch, and on each side of the premise a saddler and ironmonger.

Adam stepped back in shock, closing his eyes for a second in disbelief. When he opened them, the pharmacy and mini-mart had returned, cars driving along the high street. His own van in the bay was there, no horse and cart.

Shaking his head, he dismissed the moment as subconscious imagery guessing how the street might once have looked. Retrieving his wallet, he made for the cafe.

Inside he was greeted at the counter by a young woman wearing a striped blue and white apron.

"What would you like?" she smiled. Adam studied the chalked menu board on the wall behind her.

"Egg, bacon, beans and a slice of toast with coffee," he announced. She wrote the order on a slip of paper.

"New to these parts?" she asked, preparing to take payment. The usual cafe customers were mostly locals and she was curious about the newcomer.

"I'm staying at a cottage on the coast near Coatehaven village," he replied, handing her payment. "The villagers there are very friendly and I'm enjoying my stay."

Preparing to give him change from the till, the woman stopped for a moment.

"The Coatehaven villagers?" she queried with a puzzled frown. Adam nodded.

"Are you sure?" she pressed. Adam nodded again, wondering why she seemed doubtful.

It had happened a long time ago, but the woman knew full well from local history that Coatehaven village had disappeared into the sea with practically all inhabitants some-time back in the 1830s. Either he was mixing the place up with somewhere else, or he was a sandwich short of a picnic. Best not to press any further she thought. Some odd people passing through occasionally stopped off at the cafe. She handed him his change.

Adam detected a slight difference in the woman's body language from friendliness to wariness and wondered why. Had he offended her in some way? He let it alone and found a table by the window overlooking the high street, reassured by the view that it hadn't transformed into a different place again.

Waiting for his order he looked around the cafe. There were a few other people sitting at tables talking and eating. A large ceiling fan made an intermittent grinding noise as it slowly rotated. The tables looked clean, but the chequered black and white vinyl floor covering was faded and scored, in need of replacement.

On the cream walls were framed photographs and prints of drawings depicting the town's high street through the ages. His eyes fell on a pen and ink print. It rested between two monochrome photos on the wall facing him a few feet away. His jaw dropped in amazement.

It was the scene he'd witnessed outside a short time before. The corn merchant store, John Edwards, with sacks stacked on the porch, bordered by the ironmonger and saddlery. Adam stood up and approached to get a closer look. In the bottom right hand corner he read the artist's signature - *Robin Nesbitt*. The scene was dated 1838.

Adam was struck by the fact that on arrival he had momentarily witnessed the real high street as it was nearly two hundred years ago. The past was continuing to come alive to him in this part of the world. But why?

As he turned back to resume his seat, still puzzling over the event, he became aware of other customers looking across at him. Their attention was drawn by the gasp of surprise he'd given on seeing the drawing, a sound that he was unaware of making. Their gaze made him feel embarrassed at being the centre of interest, and he returned a sheepish smile.

He glanced outside again, wondering if the past scene had returned. Modern cars and people passed by. Perhaps the old one might return. Maybe he'd be able to walk through that former setting in the same way as he could at Coatehaven.

The thought of being able to exist in the past had advantages. He was attracted to Charlotte and wanted to know her better. He was looking forward to calling on her next day.

This happier thought was interrupted by the arrival of his breakfast. The young woman put the plate and coffee mug on the table, giving him an uncertain smile. She still wondered if the newcomer was entirely all there, especially hearing him gasp at the print on the wall for no apparent reason, as well as seeming to think Coatehaven remained intact.

******

THAT afternoon Adam returned to the village, making his way down the cobbled road towards The Ship Inn. The high street was oddly quiet with no-one in sight.

As he neared the inn, a shopkeeper opened his front door whispering something that was inaudible and waving his arm as if warning him to go back. Adam faltered, but the warning came too late. The inn door flew open and a red-coat soldier stepped out. Seeing Adam he raised his bayoneted musket and pointed the menacing weapon at him.

"Stop!" the soldier commanded. Adam froze. Several more soldiers came out of the inn, rounding on him with bayoneted muskets.

"Who are you?" the first soldier quizzed aggressively, drawing closer so the sharp point of the bayonet almost touched Adam's chest. He blurted out his name, his heart rapidly pumping in terror.

"Were you here last night when the soldiers came?" the man demanded.

Adam had no idea what to say. If he said no and someone else said they'd witnessed him here, he'd be in serious difficulty for lying. If he said yes, then a gruelling investigation would begin, and he might let slip about the carnage he'd seen to inadvertently condemn the fishermen. Terrible though that was, he didn't wish to give them away.

As he struggled to reply, Captain Abner emerged from the inn followed by his crew and several more fishermen from inside.

"He's a harmless painter!" the captain bellowed. "Leave him alone!" The men with Abner began to jeer at the soldiers. "Get out!"

Shopkeepers and more fishermen started to appear, urged on by the growing commotion.

The soldier confronting Adam lifted the bayonet away, moving back with his small group of men, all looking increasingly nervous as the swelling crowd began encircling them.

"Back away!" one of the redcoats ordered, aiming the musket anxiously, uncertain his order would be obeyed.

"Then leave us alone," the captain shouted. The soldiers realised that even armed with their weapons it wouldn't take long for the villagers to overpower them.

"If any of you had anything to do with our missing men, we'll storm the place with reinforcements," a redcoat with sergeant stripes on his tunic warned the crowd.

The villagers moved back, allowing a gap for the military party to return to their horses tethered in the yard beside the inn. As they mounted and rode off, the crowd jeered them on their way.

"I bet you need a drink after that," the captain laughed, beckoning Adam to enter the inn. The invitation was readily accepted, and he followed the fisherman and his crew inside as the villagers broke up to continue their day.

"A double measure of rum for our artist friend, Paintbrush," Abner ordered the landlord, taking coins from his trouser pocket to pay.

Adam rarely drank spirits, but the rum served to calm him. As he looked around, the scene of carnage he'd recently witnessed came back to him. But not a trace of bloodshed or damage to tables and chairs was visible. All had been cleaned or replaced.

The illicit spirit stored in the cellar below the inn had been moved to a new location. Adam dared not ask what happened to the unfortunate soldiers, but the fate of anyone who crossed the smugglers, as narrated by Charlotte and Mrs Barnaby, meant they were probably at the bottom of the sea.

"Those bastards will be back in greater numbers next time," Abner's crewmate Serious predicted as they stood drinking at the bar.

"We'll have to lay off bringing in the stuff for now," the captain's son, Tadpole, advised. They all grunted agreement.

"Don't say a word to anyone of what passes between us here," Charcoal the cook focussed on Adam with a menacing stare. Serious nodded, still harbouring suspicion that the newcomer to their group should not yet be trusted.

"I'm sure we can rely on Paintbrush to keep his mouth shut," Abner came to his defence. "After all, no-one likes swimming tied to a heavy weight." The captain expressed his oblique warning with a friendly pat on Adam's shoulder. He needed no further advice and agreed to their strict confidential terms.

Staying with the group for another rum, he listened as they discussed plans for a new inlet along the coast where they could land their illicit spirits, Serious casting occasional unnerving glances at Adam as if he was a potential traitor in their midst.

"Right we're casting off to catch the tide at two in the morning," Abner announced a little later, slamming his beer mug on the counter. "So come on men, time to get some rest."

Adam felt good as they finished their drinks, warmed not only by the alcohol, but the trust the group bestowed on him, save for the suspicious Serious.

Preparing to leave, Adam's heartbeat suddenly raced in horror. The faces of his companions had turned into skulls. Within seconds, they restored to normal, but he was panting overcome by the shock. He tottered slightly and Tadpole grabbed his arm to steady him.

"He's rummy!" Charcoal laughed and the others joined in.

"Get home and get some rest," the captain bellowed.

"Bloody city folk, can't hold their drink," a man at one of the tables called to more laughter.

Adam was recovering, though he could hardly tell them the reason for his brief unsteadiness. They would think he was not only drunk but also mad. At the door they departed, and the fishermen stood watching him for a few moments, ready to help should he fall returning along the high road.

******

BACK at the cottage, Adam wondered if Mrs Barnaby had reappeared. He checked in the living room and kitchen. Both were unoccupied, so he made his way upstairs to the bedroom.

The surprise confrontation with the soldiers and shock of seeing the skeletal faces of the fishermen, now combined with the rum to churn his stomach. He wanted to rest for a while.

Opening the bedroom door, he anticipated seeing his sleeping bag on the bedstead. Instead the neatly made bed he'd found previously had returned. Did that mean Mrs Barnaby had also returned? Since her first appearance, he hadn't looked in the second bedroom. It was empty when he'd first arrived. Was it occupied now? She had made her way upstairs to bed the previous night. Curiosity led him on.

Inside another neatly made bed met his enquiring gaze. Against the far wall stood a dark wood, mirrored dressing table with small glass pots of cream and bottles of lotion resting on it. A wardrobe with one of its double doors half-open revealed clothes hanging inside. As Adam's curiosity grew, he heard the sound of crockery being stacked down-stairs and immediately made his way to the kitchen.

"Ah, you've come back," Mrs Barnaby looked up at him, pausing from placing another plate on a stack resting on the kitchen table. The same greeting ran through Adam's mind.

"Dinner will be ready in an hour," she said, putting the plate on the pile. "Have you had a good day?"

Adam's face told otherwise. He pulled out a chair from the table and sat down, telling her about the confrontation with the soldiers. She sympathised.

"They'll be nosing around for some time now," she grumbled, turning to the work surface beside the range and picking up a knife to begin peeling potatoes.

"Did you have to go out this morning?" Adam asked, "I thought you'd told me to be here for breakfast at seven thirty, but you weren't here." The woman turned back to look at him, a puzzled expression on her face.

"You had ham, eggs and bread for breakfast. Don't you remember?"

For a second Adam doubted his senses. He had no recollection of the meal, but wondered if he may have forgotten. Mrs Barnaby shook her head.

"I think all this business with the soldiers is taking its toll on you. Perhaps you should spend more time on your painting and drawing. Relax instead of visiting the inn," she advised. "Too much alcohol isn't good for you."

Adam was certain she did not make him any breakfast, but decided it would be pointless arguing with her. Getting back to his artwork would relieve stress, especially with Charlotte by his side on their meeting tomorrow.

He left to freshen up before dinner. Entering the bedroom a new addition had appeared. By the wall opposite stood a walnut wardrobe. Mystified by its arrival, he opened the doors to see a row of clothes on brass hangers, jacket, trousers and shirts in unfamiliar style. Certainly not his own.

Confused, he looked around the room for the suitcase containing his own clothes. It was missing. His wristwatch was also gone, replaced by a silver pocket watch on the oak dresser that had now reappeared. He opened a small wooden box beside the watch. Inside were cufflinks and tie-pins.

Again his mind flew into a spin, seeming halfway between the reality he'd known and this new one invading his psyche. He rushed downstairs to the kitchen.

"Whose clothes are in that wardrobe? Why is there a pocket watch on the dresser?" he demanded furiously. Mrs Barnaby stopped stirring the pot on the range and stared at him as if he'd lost his senses.

"I've no idea what you mean?" she replied, appearing troubled by his anger. "They're all your possessions," she explained, wondering why it was necessary to do so.

Even as she spoke, Adam began to wonder what he was talking about. Of course they belonged to him. Now he started to feel a fool for making the sudden outburst.

"I'm sorry, I don't know what came over me," he lowered his head in shame. "Forgive me."

As he looked down, Adam became aware of wearing dark trousers and a frock coat, unfamiliar to him for a moment, but then swiftly he remembered they were his own.

"You need a good meal and a rest," Mrs Barnaby said, turning to stir the pot again. "That soldier business has really upset you," she tutted, shaking her head. "Now I'm preparing some fresh mackerel from today's catch at sea. Get yourself a good wash and change of clothes and you'll feel much better."

Adam thanked her for being so understanding after his rude behaviour and went back upstairs, where yet another change had taken place. The bathroom had disappeared, replaced by a storage cupboard. In the bedroom, a jug of water and bowl rested on a wooden stand for washing. Again, the change mystified him for a moment, his mind grappling to retain the former memory, but soon it accepted them as perfectly normal.

After washing he began looking in the wardrobe for clothes to wear. Reaching out to lift a garment from the rail, the sensation came over him that someone was watching from behind. He swung round.

A young man stood just inside the open door dressed in a ruffle fronted, dark red shirt and fawn trousers. Adam stared transfixed by his presence, noting the man's black, side-swept hair and horseshoe moustache. His puzzled expression equalled Adam's own confusion. He turned and left the room.

Adam crossed quickly to the door, wanting to catch up and ask what he was doing there. He looked along the landing and down the stairway. No sign of anyone. Beginning to wonder if it was another imagining he returned to the wardrobe, choosing a wing-tipped white shirt and black striped trousers to wear for dinner.

"Is there anyone else staying here?" he asked Mrs Barnaby as she served the meal in the living room.

"No," she replied, placing a plate of fresh mackerel and vegetables on the table in front of him. "Why do you ask?"

Adam was unsure about pursuing the matter further. The woman already thought he was a bit emotionally overcharged. Maybe he was. Perhaps he had been seeing things. If there were no other lodgers, she'd think him even more disturbed if he told her he'd seen a man in his room.

"Oh nothing," he replied. "I just wondered if you had another person staying here as well."

If Adam was trying to stop her thinking of him as behaving oddly, it had the opposite effect. She shook her head again, not knowing precisely why he'd asked, but surmising that something about the place was unsettling him.

"I keep telling you to relax," she said, placing over her forearm the dishcloth she'd used to carry the hot plate. "That's why you've come to my cottage to stay for a break."

The knowledge that Adam had bought the disused cottage and that he was the owner had entirely evaporated from his mind. Yes, he was here to paint and draw. To get away from it all.

While much of his former memory was slipping away, family still remained strong in his mind, and the means to communicate with his wife.

After the meal he went to his Transit parked at the front and retrieved his phone, now recharged from the earlier visit to town. The signal was weak and he had to walk a little way from the cottage for it to strengthen. He rang Josie.

"How the refurbishing going?" she asked, keen to learn of his progress in modernising the property. Adam paused before replying.

"What refurbishing?" he was puzzled by her question.

"You bought the place to do it up," she reminded him.

"No, it's Mrs Barnaby's cottage," he replied. "What makes you think I bought it? I'm just a guest."

There was a long silence as Josie tried to fathom his odd reply, almost wondering for a second if she'd misunderstood the situation.

"Who's Mrs Barnaby?" she asked, remembering he'd mentioned her before as being his landlady.

"I told you, the owner," Adam insisted.

"Are you playing some joke again," Josie sensed, even hoped, it was another silly prank like him seeing the lost village.

"No," Adam sounded annoyed. "Anyway, that's not why I rang. I was wondering if you'd bring the children down here. Maybe for a day or two? There's not a lot of room in the cottage, but I'll pay for you to stay in good accommodation nearby in the town. I'm sure the children would love being beside the sea."

"I'd have to sort out a few things first," Josie hadn't been expecting an invite for the children so soon.

"Can't you come down this weekend? I'd really love to see you all," Adam pressed.

"Well..."

"I'd be happy to speed up the divorce proceedings if you could come then," he levered.

Josie took this as moral blackmail, but she was keen to get on with the process as quickly as possible.

"I suppose I could re-arrange things so we could come on Saturday, about midday," Josie conceded, "but it would only be for one night. And don't worry about booking somewhere. I'll sort out a local hotel."

"Well if you're sure. Excellent. Looking forward to it," Adam's voice echoed triumphantly along the connection.

Josie hung up, completely mystified by his strange behaviour. She was certain he owned the cottage, so who was Mrs Barnaby? Perhaps all would become clear when she arrived with Liam and Olivia.

CHAPTER 6

A BELL clanged as Adam entered the shop where Charlotte worked. He carried the portable easel and a black case with the art materials. For the occasion he'd dressed in a puffed-sleeve white shirt, beige trousers and brown knee length boots.

There was no-one in sight and he looked at the fine collection of leather footwear on display, admiring the quality while he waited for Charlotte to appear.

After a couple of minutes a middle-aged man entered from a doorway at the back of the shop. He held a shoe and wore a white apron streaked with what looked like brown boot polish.

"Can I help you?" he asked, peering at Adam through silver rimmed spectacles under thinning strands of neatly combed-back grey hair.

"I've come for Charlotte," Adam replied, wondering if the man was her father or a workshop employee.

"Ah, she'll be along shortly," said the man, studying Adam more closely. "I presume you are staying with Mrs Barnaby," he probed.

Adam nodded.

"I'm Charlotte's father," the shopkeeper confirmed his identity. "Take a seat while you wait," he pointed the shoe, indicating a chair beside the shop counter.

"It's okay, I don't mind standing."

Adam felt slightly awkward in the presence of the man, whose eyes appeared to be weighing up his daughter's potential suitor.

"So you come from London and you're here for recreation?" Charlotte's father asked rhetorically. "And you enjoy a healthy income from your City work in commodity investments?"

Adam confirmed his situation, wondering if the man had learned about him from his daughter or just general village gossip. Another question was forming on his lips when Charlotte appeared from the back door.

"Are you being interrogated?" she smiled at Adam, then gave her father a disapproving look.

Adam was stunned by the woman's beauty. Light brown hair ringlets touched her brow and cascaded over her shoulders. She wore a long-sleeved cream blouse, black neck bow and a dark blue ankle length skirt. On her feet were black strapped shoes with side buttons. Adam wasn't sure if she should be dressed so finely for the terrain and artwork, but enjoyed seeing the sheer splendour of her womanhood.

Charlotte's father was not entirely happy that his daughter was going out for the day with a stranger to the village. By rights she should be accompanied by a female chaperone. But he'd heard good reports from the locals that Adam was a gentleman and took that on trust.

The couple left for the clifftop walk, setting down the art materials half-a-mile along the coastline to sketch a cove below. Adam was impressed by how quickly Charlotte took to the basic principles of sketching, giving advice as she worked on a pencil drawing. An hour later they were approached by a young man and woman in shorts and T-shirts carrying backpacks.

Charlotte was adding the finishing touches to her sketch as the hikers stopped to look at it.

"Waiting for inspiration are you?" the man jokingly asked Adam.

"Well Charlotte's only a beginner, but it's not a bad piece of artwork," Adam defended her efforts, annoyed by the man's remark.

The man returned a puzzled gaze, not appearing to understand Adam's sharp comment.

"What artwork?" he asked. "It's just a blank sketchpad on the easel."

Now Adam was mystified. The hikers gave him a strange look wondering if he was a nutcase. They could see neither Charlotte or her drawing. Shaking their heads they continued their walk.

"Sorry about that rude man," Adam apologised for the hiker's unwelcome remark.

"What rude man?" asked Charlotte.

"Didn't you see him?" Adam was puzzled further.

"I was probably concentrating too hard on the sketching to notice anyone," Charlotte surmised. Adam left it at that, not wishing her to think he was imagining things.

Towards the end of the day, and several more sketches completed, Adam invited Charlotte to join him in The Ship Inn. She looked offended.

"I couldn't possibly go drinking in a public house," she protested. "Only women of low virtue would do such a thing. I'm surprised you asked."

It suddenly came to Adam that in Charlotte's time mostly only serving maids or women selling sex entered alehouses.

"I'm sorry, I meant no offence," he replied, shocked at seeing her upset. She accepted the apology, understanding that he hadn't meant to offend her, and that perhaps for big city people it was normal for virtuous women to enter inns.

"But you can take me to Mrs Harcourt's tearoom in the village at eleven o'clock on Saturday," she offered the alternative. Adam was delighted. His affection for the woman was deepening.

******

"I HOPE you were a perfect gentleman today," Captain Abner greeted Adam as he entered the inn that evening. For a moment he was unsure what the fisherman meant. Then the familiar laughter of his crew drinking beer with him broke out.

Adam realised with embarrassment that word had got round of his day spent with Charlotte.

"He's turned as red as a beetroot," Charcoal commented, prompting continued laughter.

"I can assure you we spent the whole day sketching on the coastline," Adam defended himself.

"Is that what you call it?" Tadpole smirked.

"Get the man an ale," Abner called to the innkeeper, who was also enjoying the merriment.

"I'm sure he was the perfect gentleman," chimed Charcoal.

"I hope so," Serious remarked, "because people who take advantage of our young women can find themselves on a fishing trip with us." He paused for a moment. "But strangely they never return."

The veiled threat sounded all the more ominous coming from a man who Adam knew viewed him with great suspicion. It flattened the joyful atmosphere for a moment

"You've terrified the poor soul," Abner reprimanded his crewmate. The captain believed Adam wouldn't have the courage let alone motive to betray them. He considered city folk, artists and writers as inconsequential beings, and that real men were only to be found toiling on the land or at sea.

"All's well Paintbrush, we trust you to be perfectly respectable," the captain reassured him. "And that's more than I can say for the rest of the scurvy crews in this place," he shouted, looking around the inn.

He was met by good natured swearing and jibes thrown back at him by other fishermen talking and playing card games at the tables.

Several beers later Adam left the inn feeling all was right with the world. He'd promised to make drawings not only of the bay, but also a painting of the crew's fishing vessel, which pleased them. And he'd spent a wonderful day in Charlotte's company, with the prospect of soon seeing her again. How he would love to spend all his days here at Coatehaven, he reflected.

The sun had set as he stepped on to the cobblestone high road. Stars scattered the sky like sparkling grains of sugar, and the moon hovered above his cottage lighting the way ahead.

Nearing the property he stopped abruptly, catching sight of something unfamiliar in the moonlight where his van was normally parked at the front. In its place stood a horse drawn cart.

His mind struggled again between two realities of past and present. Of course, he now recalled, it was perfectly normal for the cart to be there. That's where Mrs Barnaby always kept it, harnessing the horse stabled at the back whenever she wanted to travel. Silly he should forget that. He went inside and upstairs to his comfortable bed.

Next day after breakfast he set off to do more sketching, returning to the cottage late afternoon. Entering the front door, he heard voices coming from the open kitchen doorway. Mrs Barnaby talking to a man.

About to close the front door, he saw the man come out of the kitchen and start to approach him. Adam stiffened in surprise, recognising the man as the same person who'd entered his bedroom the other day.

The figure neared, seeming unaware of another presence, then turned to climb the stairway, disappearing on the landing in the direction of Adam's room. Had Mrs Barnaby let the room to someone else while he'd been out sketching? Had he done something unwittingly to offend her?

Adam ascended the stairway while these questions ran through his head, entering the bedroom fully expecting to confront the man. But the space was unoccupied. Had this person gone into Mrs Barnaby's room instead? He was reluctant to intrude on her privacy, but curiosity drove him to open the bedroom door and look inside. That too was unoccupied save for her furniture and possessions.

Mystified, Adam returned downstairs to the kitchen, deciding to question Mrs Barnaby about the visitor who only moments ago she'd been talking to. Maybe there was a back stairway out of the cottage?

The woman was sitting at the table with her cutlery set laid out on it. In one hand she held a knife and in the other a cloth she was using to polish the utensils.

"Who's the gentleman that was in here just now?" he asked. She put down the cloth and knife, turning to face him.

"What gentleman?"

"Is there someone else staying here?" Adam continued, frustrated by the reply. He'd seen the man, heard him speaking to her, then going upstairs. He told her that.

The elderly woman shook her head.

"I think you still need to relax a little more," she smiled, picking up the knife and cloth again.

He felt patronised by the advice, but resisted making any further remark knowing the woman meant well. He was certain he'd seen the man, but then again perhaps he had imagined it. Realities seemed to slip around in his mind.

******

ADAM could hardly contain his excitement a few days later, as he made his way down the village high street to meet Charlotte in Mrs Harcourt's tearoom.

For the special occasion he'd selected from the bedroom wardrobe a wine red tailcoat, check waistcoat, white shirt with maroon bow-tie, and cream breeches. He intended to impress the woman he was now intent on making his own.

The tearoom was situated down a cobbled side road off the main street. Outside the sign above - 'Mrs Harcourt's - was neatly scripted in italic gold lettering on a dark brown hoarding. White lace curtains curved inwards at each end of the wide glass frontage.

Adam entered to the clang of a doorbell. Well dressed men and women sat at several tables. Unlit oil lamps in brass holders were spaced along the floral papered walls.

A woman stopped stacking plates behind the dark wood counter and approached Adam. She was middle-aged and wore a crisp, white apron over the portly spread of her long green dress. Her grey hair was tied neatly in a bun.

"Can I help you sir?" she smiled from a face generously powdered white to hide traces of time. Heavily rouged lips seemed to leap from their pale background.

Not seeing Charlotte in the tearoom, Adam explained he was expecting her and asked for a table. The woman led him to seating by the front window.

While waiting he glanced around the setting, noting the fine clothes of the other patrons. They didn't have weathered faces like the working villagers and obviously came from wealthier parts of the district. The place would be strictly off-limits to the likes of Captain Abner and crew, thought Adam, and must have some unique reputation for quality to attract upmarket people. Likely they would never come to the village at night.

Wondering how much longer Charlotte would be, he glanced out the window to see if she was approaching. His heart skipped a beat. Walking past was the man who kept making mysterious appearances in the cottage.

Adam sprang towards the door to confront him and almost collided with Charlotte entering.

"Sorry." He pulled back sharply.

"What's the matter?" she cried.

"Just a moment," he slipped past her into the street.

The mystery man was nearing a corner. Adam ran to catch up. The figure disappeared around the corner. Adam swiftly followed, rounding it. The man was nowhere to be seen.

A couple of women stood chatting, otherwise the side street was empty.

"Did you see a man pass you just a moment ago?" he asked. They stared quizzically at him and shook their heads. It seemed the figure had yet again disappeared into thin air.

Adam returned to Charlotte full of apologies as she stood outside the tearoom baffled by his behaviour.

"What on earth is the matter?"

"I'm sorry," Adam apologised yet again. "There's a man who keeps appearing and disappearing," he replied. She stared still none the wiser as to what he meant.

"Let's go inside and I'll explain," he opened the door, now noticing that in the rush he'd had no time to see how stunning she looked, wearing a dark blue bustle dress, and those wonderful ringlets spilling beneath the rim of her light-blue bonnet with a bright yellow band around it

"You look absolutely beautiful," he told her, as they sat at the table with a pot of tea and selection of cakes. Her soft face reddened. She glanced down for a moment, both pleased and embarrassed by the compliment. But she was intrigued by his strange behaviour chasing after someone in the street. Adam described the man, dark side-combed hair and horseshoe moustache, and the little else that he knew beside the appearances.

"Every time I try to question him, the man disappears," Adam declared in frustration. "He's either an amazing escape artist or a ghost."

Charlotte said nothing for a moment as Adam forked a piece of sponge cake on his plate and lifted it to his mouth. He wondered if she thought he'd imagined the sightings or was deranged.

Finally, her reaction was not entirely what he expected. Her eyes had been steeped in thought.

"Your description of him nudges something in my memory," she replied, "but I can't quite place it. I'm certain I've seen the man, perhaps even met him, though as I say, it's not coming to mind right now."

Adam waited a moment, hoping she might recall something more. But none came.

"Sorry," she said, truly wishing to help.

"Well if anything else occurs to you, let me know," Adam urged. Charlotte nodded.

"Of one thing I'm fairly certain," she added, "it wasn't a ghost." She laughed, making light of such a ridiculous suggestion. Adam laughed too, coming to the conclusion there must be some rational explanation to the man's disappearances.

The conversation turned to Charlotte's life in the village and how she yearned to travel further afield. But since her mother had died of the consumption when Charlotte was only twelve, and there being no other children, she was duty bound to help her father run the footwear business.

Her desire to travel led Adam to ask if she would like to visit places with him. Charlotte warmed to the idea, but thought the suggestion rather forward coming from someone she hadn't known long. She'd be frowned upon for taking off with a man who was largely a stranger to the village. And her father would not only be angered, he'd have great difficulty running the shop on his own. She explained the problem.

Adam fell silent for a while and sipped tea, wondering if he should say what he was thinking. He came to a decision.

"I'm very fond of you," he paused. "In fact, to be honest, I've fallen in love with you and would like you to become my wife."

Charlotte's face reddened more deeply than when he'd complimented her earlier. She was lost for words. The offer of marriage was completely unexpected. She too was strongly attracted to him, but they hadn't known each other long. His was a city world. She was a fishing village woman.

"Perhaps we should spend more time together first," she eventually replied.

"I'm wealthy. If it's your father you're worried about, I could provide staffing for him, even set up him up in a town where his business would flourish," Adam attempted to persuade her. "You could live with me in comfort, travel abroad, as well as see your father as often as you liked."

The offer was hugely tempting. Charlotte needed time to assess the monumental changes it would bring to her life. She'd been expecting a simple meeting over tea and cakes.

"I think we should wait," she smiled softly. Adam realised he was rushing her too much. The couple said nothing for a moment.

"Would you like more tea?" the tearoom lady stood by their table.

"Yes please Mrs Harcourt," Charlotte looked up. Adam nodded, now realising the woman who'd greeted him on arrival was the owner.

"I'll make you a new infusion then." She took the teapot.

The couple remained silent a little longer, the potency of Adam's proposal still clinging in the air.

"Perhaps we could become engaged as a first step," Adam broke the silence. Charlotte glanced down, still racked with emotional turmoil, then looked up at him.

"I do appreciate your generous offer, but still think we should wait."

Adam was deeply disappointed with the reply, though felt it wasn't the moment to press any further. Another time he decided.

Mrs Harcourt returned with the tea and they began talking about painting and drawing. Suddenly it occurred to Adam that Josie and children were due that afternoon. He also realised that he would certainly need to speed up divorce proceedings if he wanted to marry Charlotte.

Hurriedly he explained the position to her, assuring there would be no obstacle if she consented to marry him. Now Charlotte was entirely bemused and definitely felt the need to consider her future.

"I'd love you to meet my son and daughter. They should be arriving any time now," Adam glanced at his pocket watch.

Reluctantly Charlotte agreed. She hadn't bargained for introductions to Adam's newly announced family, but was curious to see the others involved in his life.

CHAPTER 7

JOSIE parked her car on the overgrown cobblestone road running past the cottage with Liam and Olivia sitting in the back.

They climbed out of the vehicle and the children stood staring at the rundown state of the property, missing roof tiles, dark discoloured patches indicating damp on the flint stone walls, and weeds growing out of cracks in the fabric.

"Dad's got a lot of work to do," observed eleven-year-old Liam, dressed in a red sports top and shorts. The brown-haired boy gave his mum a wry grin.

"It isn't a very big place," sneered his nine-year-old sister, a grimace forming on her freckled face. "I don't think I'd like to live in it." She wore a short-sleeved, yellow dress with white lace edging. The girl began approaching the cottage, her long auburn hair flowing over her back.

"Yes, let's go and see dad," said Josie, following her daughter and ignoring the children's comments, though she didn't disagree with them. For the visit she'd dressed in a long-sleeved white top and light grey trousers.

Knocking on the front door, Josie was surprised that Adam hadn't already come out to greet them. She'd also found it odd that he'd failed to respond to her phone calls in the last couple of days to confirm the visit was still on. Maybe the signal hadn't got through. Not hearing from him she'd presumed it was okay to come.

Now receiving no reply to several knocks, she turned the handle to find the door unlocked. They stepped into the dark hallway, the walls browned with age, the bare wood stairway.

"Dad hasn't done much here," said Liam disapprovingly.

Josie called out to her husband, but there was no reply. Had she got the wrong day? Maybe something had happened that made him leave in a hurry, although his Transit van was still parked on the gravel frontage.

She entered the kitchen with the children. Dirty plates with decaying remnants of food lay on the table. A cereal bowl with traces of dried cornflakes rested on the counter beside the range. Cutlery submerged in the greyed water of a washing-up bowl lay in the sink. Flies skirted around the room, settling back on a plate with mouldy meat remnants after being disturbed by the visitors entering.

"Urrr," said Olivia. She peered at her mother, looking appalled.

"Has dad made this mess?" asked Liam, hardly able to believe it could be so. Josie was certain that he had, but again voiced no opinion.

Upstairs, Adam's sleeping bag rested on the thin mattress of the old bedstead, clothes heaped in a pile on the wooden floorboards. The smaller second bedroom was completely empty.

"Where's dad?" asked Liam. "Are you sure this is the right place?"

Josie knew it was, but again said nothing.

"I think he's forgotten we were coming," disappointment was palpable in Olivia's tone.

They descended the stairs into the hallway again, and as Josie was preparing to ring Adam the front door opened and he appeared.

"So sorry I'm a bit late," he entered smiling, opening his arms to hug the children. They recoiled, their mouths wide open in shock.

"What's the matter?" he stared in surprise. "I said I'm sorry for being late."

Josie was in a state of shock too. Her husband's blue check shirt and black jeans were filthy, food stains and patches of dusty dirt spread liberally all over them. An unkempt beard was forming on his usually clean shaven face, his dark hair matted.

"What have you been doing to yourself?" Josie cried. "You look a wreck!"

Adam was totally mystified. He looked at his clothing and saw the smart outfit he'd chosen for meeting Charlotte. He had groomed himself to look his very best. What was Josie talking about?

Ignoring his wife's comment for a moment, he turned to introduce Charlotte standing just behind him. Josie and the children stared blankly.

"There's no-one there daddy," said Olivia.

Adam took Charlotte's hand for her to stand beside him, thinking he might be obscuring his family's view of the woman.

"There's no-one there," said Charlotte.

Now Adam was totally bemused. Apparently his wife and children couldn't see her, and she couldn't see them.

"I'd better be getting back home," Charlotte decided, wondering if he was playing a silly game. Given the strangeness of the situation Adam thought it best not to persuade her otherwise.

"I'll be in touch. Perhaps we can do more drawing together?" he suggested hopefully. Charlotte nodded and left.

"Who are you talking to?" Josie was growing more concerned than ever with his odd behaviour.

"Charlotte Robson, a woman I met in the village," he replied, still puzzled as to why Josie and the children hadn't seen her. He decided to change the subject, wanting this to be a happy occasion.

"I expect you're all hungry after the long journey," he said. "Mrs Barnaby has gone into town to buy provisions, but she should be back shortly to make us some lunch."

"Who is this Mrs Barnaby you keep talking about?" Josie insisted, growing frustrated by his constant mention of the mystery woman.

"The owner of the cottage. She's my housekeeper while I'm staying here. I've told you before." Adam was equally frustrated by his wife's constant questioning about her.

"But you own the bloody place! Oops!" Josie put her hand to her mouth, realising she'd used a word that she hadn't meant to use in front of the children.

"I don't own the place," he raised his voice. "I'm renting it for a break. Why don't you believe me?"

For a moment there was an embarrassed silence in the terse atmosphere.

"Come on, your here to have some fun," Adam steered the conversation away from the disagreement. "Let's go outside and I'll show you some wonderful views along the clifftops. And after we've eaten I can take you to see fishing boats at the seafront."

Josie wasn't aware of any seafront with boats in the locality, but she presumed it must be nestled below the clifftop further along the coastline with access down to it.

Adam led them across the gravel frontage to the old road leading to the cliff edge.

"I've just remembered, David asked me to call and let him know we've arrived safely," said Josie, reaching into her handbag and taking out her phone. "You lot go on and I'll catch you up in a minute."

Adam looked puzzled, wondering how she would let her partner know with the strange object she'd taken from her bag. Then he shrugged his shoulders, more intent on enjoying the company of his children. After getting over the initial shock of his unkempt appearance, they readily took his hands as he led them forward.

"I know," he said, "let's go for a walk into the village, and I'll take you down to the seafront now. No point in waiting until after we've eaten." They walked on a little further.

"Where is this village?" asked Olivia, seeing only a cliff edge and the sea beyond in their direction as they drew nearer.

"There!" he nodded ahead. "Can't you see the cottages along the high street?"

"There aren't any cottages," exclaimed Liam, confirming their absence.

"You'll see them in a moment," Adam began tugging his children's hands as they started to resist going any further.

"We'd better stop soon," Olivia cried, "we're getting a bit close to the edge."

"Nonsense, we'll be in the high street shortly. Can't you see the people walking around?"

Olivia and Liam could not. Only the end of the cliff that they were now dangerously close to plunging over. They desperately resisted going further, but their hands were clasped in their father's iron grip.

Josie stood on the gravel frontage looking towards the cottage as she phoned David. After telling him of their safe arrival, she went on to describe Adam's strange behaviour.

"I'm not keen on staying for long, and it's just as well we're booked into a local hotel. The cottage is a complete tip and he still keeps imagining things." She turned and looked towards Adam and the children. Her jaw widened in horror. The phone fell from her hand seeing the youngsters struggling to escape as they neared the cliff drop.

"For Christ's sake, you maniac!" she screamed at the top of her voice, springing like a tiger.

"Stop daddy! Stop!" the youngsters shouted, desperate to free themselves from their father's grasp with the edge just feet away. He ignored their pleas, confident they'd soon be entering the village ahead.

"Stop you fucking maniac!" Josie yelled in full flight, fearing any second the children would be hurtling downwards to their doom on the beach below. Her legs felt leaden, desperately trying to reach them.

The children pulled back with all their strength, but it only slightly slowed Adam's onward progress. They could see him raising his leg to step over the edge and began screaming in terror.

Next second they felt themselves being forcefully tugged back, panic lending superhuman power to Josie as she grabbed their clothing from behind. The force wrenched Adam back.

"Let go of them you fucking madman!" screamed Josie. Hearing her and totally thrown by her fury, Adam instantly released them. The children swung round into their mother's open arms, crying but deeply relieved to nestle into her safety.

"What the hell are you doing?" Josie demanded venomously, as she started drawing the youngsters further back from him. Adam stared, genuinely confused and hurt.

"I was just taking them down to the village seafront. Show them the fishing boats," he replied innocently. "I might ask why you're behaving so weirdly?"

"There is no bloody village you keep harping on about. It's a cliff edge with just the beach below," Josie yelled, her panic now welling into rage. "You nearly killed them!"

"There's the village," said Adam, turning and pointing at the void. "Surely you can see it?"

Josie could not and neither the children. She shook her head in despair. Her husband was not right in the head. Something strange had happened to him since he'd arrived in this place.

"Look. I'll show you the village is there," Adam was determined to prove his point. He faced the cliff and began the few paces forward.

"No don't!" Josie and the children pleaded.

As he reached the edge, a thick sea mist suddenly swirled upwards, totally blotting out view of the cliff-side and sea beyond. Adam disappeared into it.

"Daddy!" the children yelled, met by silence. They stood transfixed in horror, fearing he'd fallen to his death, but unable to see in the mist. Josie began to go a little way into its shroud to check if her husband might just be standing on the edge. But she couldn't risk misjudging her steps and toppling over. She backed away.

Tears streamed from Liam and Olivia's eyes as they started to cry. Josie did her best to comfort them, guiding them away from the scene.

"Now does that prove it?" boomed Adam's voice from behind. "You must have seen me enter the high street."

They turned as he emerged from the mist, their eyes wide in amazement.

He beamed triumphantly, apparently unaware of there being any mist. When he started to approach them, the vapour swirled for a moment then completely evaporated as swiftly as it had come.

The children ran to him, thrilled and relieved their father was still alive. He hugged them tightly, thinking they were now satisfied with proof the village existed. Josie too was deeply relieved he hadn't perished, but the feeling was tempered with ongoing doubt about his sanity.

It was odd the sea mist suddenly appearing and disappearing, but such phenomena was not unknown in coastal areas. And seafarers were often exposed to mists quickly rising. Adam probably just stood at the edge, she surmised. Though she still couldn't dismiss the fact it was strange the mist should suddenly appear at that moment. Logic, however, was not her priority. She didn't want to risk the children's safety any further and desired to get them away as fast as possible.

"Come on, we're going home now," she called to the youngsters. For a moment they appeared reluctant, continuing to hug their father in relief at seeing him unharmed. But they knew it was unwise to disobey their mother's wishes.

"Why are you leaving?" Adam again seemed baffled by his wife's inexplicable behaviour.

Josie no longer wanted to call him insane to his face. She now realised he was genuinely suffering from some psychiatric disorder.

"All the hotels were booked, I was going to tell you," she lied. "So we can only make it a short visit." Josie knew it didn't sound a convincing excuse, but it would have to do.

"Well this is ridiculously short, you've only just arrived," Adam protested as the children released him and approached their mother. He'd offer his own bedroom for Josie and sleep downstairs himself in the living room, but he could hardly turf Mrs Barnaby out for the children.

"I'll see if I can find a room at The Ship Inn for you," he began.

"No. We'd better be getting back now," Josie insisted.

Short of holding them hostage, Adam could do no more in persuading her to stay. He knew from their previous relationship together that she was stickler when her mind was made up.

They returned to the cottage and the youngsters gave their father another hug before getting into the car.

"I'll be in touch," said Josie, stooping to pick up the phone she dropped earlier in the panic. There was a recorded message from David, probably wondering why the call to him had cut off abruptly. She'd check it later. Her priority was to put some distance from the place. Adam stared, trying to figure out the rectangular object she held in her hand.

Josie climbed into the car and the children waved to him as she pulled away. Adam waved back, seeing Liam and Olivia sitting on the rear seat of an open carriage, with Josie at the front holding the horse's reins.

CHAPTER 8

THE next morning Adam made his way down to the seafront to sketch some of the sailing vessels. Halfway along the high street the ground briefly shook a little, making him side-step a couple of times to keep balance.

He remembered it happening before when he was with Charlotte. But she'd been unaware of the event, as well as the lightning and thunder clap accompanying it. At present the sky was clear except for a few puffy white clouds. Good weather for sketching he thought, though the earth tremor was a bit unsettling.

He sat on a bench at the seafront wall with the sketch pad resting on his lap, and began drawing a tall sail ship moored at the end of a pier. Smaller craft and rowing boats bobbed in the water below.

Every so often fishermen passing by would stop to look at his artwork, some praising it and others just grunting before moving on. After an hour of sketching he looked up hearing a familiar voice greet him. Charlotte stood beside the bench dressed in a sober black dress and bonnet.

"That's a wonderful drawing," she complimented the work, bringing a smile to Adam's face. "I've been to church and thought I'd take a stroll down here."

Adam was thrilled to see her. He stopped sketching and stood up.

"Don't stop for me," she said.

"It's alright I've done enough," he replied, putting the pencil away in a small case resting on the bench and closing the sketch pad.

For a moment he was lost for more words, coyly remembering the incident yesterday when he introduced her to his family who she apparently couldn't see. The event still mystified him, and he wasn't sure how he could offer Charlotte an explanation for what must have seemed strange behaviour.

"I must apologise....," he began, struggling for a rational answer, perhaps even a white lie.

"I have to say I was really annoyed by you playing that stupid joke on me yesterday," Charlotte interrupted. "What was the point pretending you were seeing your family?"

Adam faltered to reply.

"Do you actually have a family or not? Are really married?" Charlotte seemed more concerned with establishing that fact than the charade she believed he'd played.

"Yes, I do," Adam insisted, "but I'm divorcing my wife as I told you."

Charlotte glared at him for a while as if making a decision.

"Well if you want to keep seeing me, please do not play any more silly games like that," she firmly stated her terms. Then her glaring gaze softened.

Adam felt duly humiliated and relieved their relationship could continue without further explanation needed. He couldn't provide one if she did.

"Would you like a cup of tea at Mrs Harcourt's?" he asked as a peace offering. Charlotte smiled agreement.

Over cucumber sandwiches and tea Adam told her of his intention to start painting scenes of the bay and portraits of characters like Captain Abner. Charlotte pulled a face at mention of the fishermen's name, knowing his ways hid a totally ruthless nature beneath the hearty exterior.

The conversation fell silent for a while. Charlotte seemed to be struggling to put her thoughts into words. Finally she spoke.

"Yesterday you asked me if we could become engaged," her voice tailed off for a second or two. "I've given it some thought, but of course you are still married." She paused again, now looking flustered. Adam broke in to save her from the awkward moment.

"I'm going to be divorced soon, as I've told you. If you'll take me, perhaps we could become unofficially engaged," he suggested, "a secret for now between just us." Adam reached across the table, placing his palm softly on her left hand. Charlotte smiled.

"My father would have to be informed. I'm not sure how he would take it. I'd prefer his blessing," she said. Adam agreed, but feared it might be a stumbling block.

"I'll buy you an engagement ring tomorrow," he promised, "you can keep it to wear after your father has been told."

"Our secret until then," Charlotte whispered, after considering the proposition for a few moments.

"Would you like more tea?" Mrs Harcourt interrupted, finishing wiping clean the empty table beside them. From the knowing gleam in her eyes, Adam felt sure the woman had overheard their intimate conversation.

"No, I must return home," said Charlotte, "father will wonder why I've been delayed from church."

Adam paid Mrs Harcourt and the couple made their way to the door. As they left, Adam looked back at the woman, who'd returned behind the counter. She still had the knowing gleam as she glanced back at him. Her face suddenly transformed into a skull, empty eye sockets coldly staring.

Adam gasped, recoiling in horror and bumping into Charlotte at the open doorway.

"What's the matter?" she cried, turning in surprise.

As he looked again, Mrs Harcourt's face had returned to the gleam.

"Nothing, I'm alright," he replied, swiftly gathering his wits. She'd hardly believe what he'd seen, and would think he was now playing an even worse joke if he told her.

He accompanied his newly betrothed along the high street towards her father's shop, taking care to avoid the fish carts clattering up and down the road.

Nearing the premises, the ground began to shake a little. This time Charlotte also felt the tremor.

"Does that happen often?" asked Adam.

"Very occasionally," she said. "It's just a bit of ground settlement. Nothing to worry about." Adam was not so sure. There was something in the back of his mind that troubled him about it, but accepted Charlotte's local knowledge as being correct. They walked on for a few more minutes, stopping in the alley outside the shop's rear door.

"Now that we're secretly engaged, perhaps my fiancée would permit me to give her a kiss," Adam ventured.

Charlotte blushed, then peered each way along the alley to make sure no-one else was in sight. She leaned forward to meet Adam's lips in a soft kiss, which began to passionately increase as they embraced. Charlotte broke away, sacrificing pleasure for fear of someone entering the alley and seeing them. Even worse, her father suddenly opening the door and catching them. He'd be furious at intimacy that had no official status, especially involving his own daughter. The shame.

"When can you come sketching again?" asked Adam.

"I have Wednesday afternoon free," she replied.

"I'll call for you."

They kissed quickly again before Charlotte entered the shop.

******

THAT evening Adam was greeted by a noisy chorus as he opened the door of The Ship Inn. Abner and crew had not long returned from a three-day fishing excursion and were making the most of boosting their ale and spirit intake.

"Here comes the lover!" the captain shouted to a round of laughter from the regulars.

Adam was briefly thrown off-guard, wondering what Abner meant. Then it dawned on him that Mrs Harcourt, overhearing his intimate conversation with Charlotte in the tearoom, had likely spread the news of their secret engagement.

"She's a fine girl," the captain commended, "you make sure you treat her well."

Adam had every intention of doing so, and soon with a beer in hand, he joined in the general banter, realising it was now pointless to hide the fact of his engagement.

A short time later the inn door opened and an elderly bearded man entered, dressed in a white smock, bucket hat and knee length brown boots. All eyes fixed on him.

"Why it's mad Sam the shepherd man," the captain's son Tadpole announced, his words slightly slurred from the alcohol. "What brings you here?"

"To warn you all of impending doom," the man growled. Laughter broke out.

Seeing him reminded Adam of the mysterious encounter outside the cottage when he'd first arrived. This was the person who'd said something to him about impossibly real, couched as if it was some sort of warning. He couldn't remember precisely.

"You're always foretelling some terrible fate or other," Tadpole smirked. "Come and have a drink and relax old man. You've retired now. Enjoy yourself." He beckoned the elderly man to join the group.

"Enjoy your drink while you may," replied the intruder on their company, wagging his finger at them. "I've seen the future."

"He doesn't need a drink to start seeing things," Charcoal piped in, encouraging another round of laughter.

The old man ignored the insults, now concentrating a grim gaze on Adam.

"You would do well to return to your own world, my friend," he advised. "Time is short. The impossible has endless possibilities."

The enigmatic warning sent a chill through Adam, but he was puzzled. Surely this was his world? Coatehaven.

The retired shepherd turned and left. The regulars shook their heads, smiling in the firm belief that the man was unhinged.

By the end of the evening Adam was in high spirits after consuming several more beers and a rum or two. He swayed as he made his way back to the cottage. The ground shook briefly again, but he was unsure if he'd imagined the tremor, or was just unsteady from the effect of alcohol.

Mrs Barnaby greeted him in the lamp-lit hallway when he arrived back. Her expression was grim.

"Charlotte's father has been here," she announced. "He's furious with you."

"Why?" Adam quickly sobered up.

"Said you've no right to become engaged to his daughter without asking him for consent first."

Adam cursed Mrs Harcourt under his breath. The tearoom owner had obviously spread the overheard conversation far and wide.

"I'll go and see him first thing tomorrow, set things straight," he told his landlady. She nodded agreement. Now Adam felt overwhelmingly tired. The high spirits knocked out of him, he began making his way upstairs to bed.

"Congratulations," Mrs Barnaby called to him with a smile when he was halfway up the stairway. He smiled back half-heartedly.

******

CHARLOTTE appeared troubled when Adam entered the shop next morning. She knew exactly why he'd come, and they didn't need to exchange a word about the matter as she led him to the workshop at the back.

Her father sat at a long wooden table wearing a brown leather apron and hammering tacks into the sole of a boot. He continued working for a while, leaving Adam to suffer silent penitence and wonder what fury awaited him.

After a few minutes the man stopped hammering and looked up, scrutinising Adam for a little longer before speaking.

"I was extremely angry at being the last person, it would seem, to learn of your engagement to my daughter," he began, falling silent again for a moment.

"Charlotte has since explained to me that she believes Mrs Harcourt overheard your private conversation and recklessly spread the word around the village. And that you both had every intention to speak first to me about the matter."

Adam started to reply, but the man raised his hand to stop him.

"So in that case, I will forgive you. However, you should have sought my consent before offering any pledge of matrimony to my daughter," he lectured.

"I apologise, but I do love your daughter," Adam uttered, looking at Charlotte standing beside him. She blushed.

"That's as may be," her father replied," but I will need to see you are truly committed to her." The man feared his daughter might suffer disappointment and shame if this relative stranger led her astray and then deserted. On the other hand he knew Adam was wealthy and able to give her a good lifestyle.

The man stood up and approached Adam, a stern expression on his face.

"I will give my blessing to your marriage on condition that you remain resident in this area for a year beforehand," he announced his decision.

Adam was thrilled. He had grown attached to Coatehaven and the condition would be no hardship for him. Agreement reached they shook hands. Charlotte was overjoyed, but resisted the urge to kiss her future husband in front of her father.

"Now dear, you must get back to your duties in the shop," he instructed her.

"I'll see you on Wednesday afternoon," she said to Adam and left.

Her father returned to his work. Adam stood awkwardly for a moment before realising his presence was no longer required. On his way out he passed his fiancée serving a customer in the shop.

Over the next few weeks, whenever she was free, the couple spent time walking, painting, drawing and visiting the teashop, where Charlotte had given Mrs Harcourt a piece of her mind.

On most evenings Adam enjoyed a drink at the inn, which also gave him the opportunity to settle better with the locals, even Serious beginning to accept him. Charlotte was required to remain in the home at this time, and certainly couldn't and wouldn't enter the premises.

Thoughts of family began to fade, as Adam immersed himself further into the ways of Coatehaven.

******

WHILE Adam had all but entirely forgotten about the modern world, his wife Josie increasingly thought of him. He hadn't responded to her calls for weeks. She even wrote him a letter, but received no reply.

He'd looked in a dreadful state when she'd visited with the children, and she was worried he may have become incapably ill in the cottage. Certainly his mind appeared unbalanced. Had he perhaps attempted to enter that long lost village again and fallen over the edge of the cliff? Laying dead, perhaps, unnoticed?

Josie's partner was growing irritated by her concern. He wished Adam was no longer part of their life and his main interest in the lack of communication was the delay it might cause to the divorce proceedings.

Another week passed, and as Josie's concern continued to increase, she decided to do some research on the history of the former fishing village, as well as considering another visit if Adam remained out of touch for much longer.

"Perhaps you could speed up the divorce by citing your husband's insanity," David commented sarcastically one evening. He was sitting on the living room sofa watching TV, while Josie beside him scrolled for information on her laptop about the old east coast village.

She ignored his unkind remark, understanding her partner's frustration and how he viewed Adam as a continuing obstacle to their marrying and moving on.

Her search seemed only to turn up a few references to Coatehaven, mainly a brief paragraph or two of it disappearing into the sea. Beginning to give up hope of any detailed information, she suddenly came across a website hosted by a local historian living in the area. The site proved to be a rich vein of knowledge, dating events far back in its fishing village history.

The more she read, the greater her anxiety grew. Thoughts that at first seemed ludicrous began to colour her imagination. Surely not, she asked herself time and again, attempting without success to dismiss them.

She dared not voice her thoughts to David. He'd laugh her out of the room. She could guess his disbelief, and probably he'd be right.

But that night strange images raced through Josie's head. She slept fitfully, waking frequently and mumbling in her sleep. David's initial sympathy for her unrest started to wear thin, with incoherent chatter constantly waking him.

Finally she got up in the early morning to avoid disturbing him again, and made herself a cup of tea in the kitchen. As she sipped the brew, she came to a decision.

"Why on earth are you going to drive down there now?" David asked later, as they sat together at the kitchen table eating breakfast. He was annoyed and puzzled. Now Josie felt duty bound to tell him, and just as she had anticipated he fell about laughing.

"I think you're going as mad as him," he said, as his laughter subsided.

"Never mind, I'm going there. I should be back by this evening." Josie stuck to her decision. "Tell the children where I've gone when they're up. And remember it's their Sunday swimming club at ten o'clock."

David shook his head, resigned to her will.

CHAPTER 9

THE weather had been kind for much of the time, and Adam had been able to take advantage of mostly dry days for outdoor painting and sketching.

Now the elements had turned, so that more often he was confined to the cottage pursuing his art. When Charlotte wasn't working, she joined him, adding to her own artwork skills.

On Adam's part he had a growing desire to bed her, and sometimes they enjoyed intimate kissing and exploring when Mrs Barnaby was out. But the prize for him was not yet on offer.

"When we are married," Charlotte would insist, fighting back her own desire for fulfilment. Strength to resist was strongly reinforced by the spectre of her father. Should she arrive at the altar carrying a child, the shame and his fury would be unbearable.

Charlotte left the cottage late one afternoon, wearing a blue scarf and black cloak to protect herself from the blustery wind and drizzle that had gone on for several days.

Adam felt hungry, and while Mrs Barnaby was in town visiting a relative, he went to the kitchen to see if he could find one of her delicious tarts filled with redcurrant preserve. He was lucky, she'd made a fresh batch that morning and had stored them in the larder. He helped himself to one.

Leaving the kitchen and entering the hallway, he was about to take a bite when the front door began opening. For a second he thought it was Mrs Barnaby returning. Instead the shape of a man appeared. That man! The stranger he'd seen in his room and in the village. The one who kept mysteriously disappearing.

"Who are you?" Adam bellowed, staring aggressively at the man with the black side-combed hair and horseshoe moustache. The stranger appeared not to notice him. He closed the door and made his way upstairs. Adam stood mesmerised for a moment, stunned by the sheer cheek of the man entering the cottage without permission or invite. Anger welled. He raced up the stairs, this time totally determined to confront him. But a search of the rooms showed no trace of his presence.

Slowly it dawned on Adam that he may have seen a ghost. It could be the only explanation. No living person could disappear completely in the little time it took to search upstairs. But who was this apparent apparition?

He didn't dare question Mrs Barnaby again on the matter. She'd already given him peculiar looks when he'd asked about this man, spectre, whatever.

That evening the drizzle had cleared, and as Adam made his way along the high street to his favourite watering hole for company, the fading watery sunset on the horizon didn't hold much hope for dry weather to come.

"They're at sea," the innkeeper greeted him as he entered, guessing that Adam was seeking the crew's companionship.

"Let's hope they get back safely," a grey bearded man wearing a mariner's cap and gansey jumper called to the landlord. He sat at a table playing cards with a younger group of fishermen. "All the signs of a big storm brewing," the man continued, "and I reckon from my many years at sea, a force 11 is on the way. A bloody terrible beast to reckon with out there."

"There's Josiah and his crew out there too," one of the younger men reminded him. The group nodded and grunted agreement for the fishermen's safe return.

Adam felt out of place in the setting. These were men who knew true physical hardship and danger to earn a mere pittance. His wealth had been acquired without any risk to his well-being. But they didn't consider Adam an outsider, especially since he was marrying into the village, and invited him to play cards with them. Their acceptance was worth a great deal to him.

******

THE following morning Adam was surprised to see bright sunlight flooding into the bedroom as he drew back the curtains. Even old sea salts can be wrong about the weather he thought.

The sky was clear blue, perfect for sketching, and after breakfast he set off with a couple of pads and a set of pencils to record more bay scenes. As arranged, Charlotte joined him at the end of Sunday service, and they sat together on the waterside bench among the bustle of fishermen repairing nets, scrubbing decks and off-loading catches from their vessels into carts.

A couple of hours passed when a fishing boat came into view and berthed at the pier. Adam recognised Captain Abner and his men setting to work unloading their catch. Then they covered equipment on the deck with tarpaulins. When they'd finished the crew came along the pier, and seeing the couple Abner greeted them in his usual bullish way.

"Why it's the lover sweethearts," he laughed. Charlotte turned away in embarrassment. Adam smiled, embarrassed too, but knowing the captain well enough to realise it was well intentioned.

"We're off for a drink before we get our heads down, d'ye fancy coming?" he invited Adam. The invite was declined. Right now he much preferred the company of his future wife.

"We won't be going out to sea again for a while, there's one hell of a storm on its way," said Abner, "so time to batten down the hatch at The Ship Inn for a day or two." He laughed again heartily and made for the high street followed by his crew.

The captain's comment about the weather surprised Adam. Now he and the old man at the inn had predicted an approaching storm. But the sky still looked peacefully blue and settled. No sign of anything adverse in sight. They'd obviously got it wrong.

It was late afternoon when he noticed a change, a darkening far out on the horizon.

Charlotte was putting the finishing touches to the sails of a moored smack she was sketching, when it became apparent that the distant, deep grey cloud spreading across the horizon was starting to approach.

Fishermen began lowering the sails on their vessels and covering deck equipment with tarpaulins. Perhaps Abner and the old man were right about the weather thought Adam as he and Charlotte prepared to leave.

While making their way up the cobblestone slope towards Charlotte's home, a strong gust of wind struck, nearly knocking them off their feet. Thick dark cloud raced towards the village swirling and blotting out the sky with raindrops now pounding into the couple.

The wind whipped into a howl, and as Adam glanced back at the seafront he could see high waves furiously battering the two jetties, foaming spray scattering across their length. Sailing vessels rocked helplessly at their moorings, with some of the small boats anchored mid bay flipping over in the turbulence. Fishermen scurried up the slope to find protection in their homes or at the inn. There was nothing further they could do right now to save their vessels from the onslaught.

So rapid was the storm's arrival that by the time Adam and Charlotte reached the door of the shop, thick grey cloud shrouded the village in near darkness. Lamps being lit in the cottages began shining through windows.

"Come inside," said Charlotte as she opened the shop door. "Hopefully it'll blow itself out soon."

Adam had intended to make his way back to Mrs Barnaby's, but the invite was welcome. Their clothes were already soaked.

"Come into the living room and I'll make us a hot drink." Charlotte was starting to shiver slightly from the cold rainwater penetrating her black dress.

Strong wind struck the shop front window, hammering rain into it sideways. A flash of lightning lit the street, swiftly followed by a crack of thunder as the couple made their way into the living room. They were greeted by Charlotte's father.

"Thought you'd soon be back," he said to Charlotte, rising from an armchair by the fireside. He glanced at Adam, not entirely sure that he should have entered the interior without his invitation. But the weather was vicious. He'd make an exception on protocol.

"This one's settling in for a while," the man continued, approaching a window overlooking the back yard. The large shed where he kept his work tools was almost obscured from view by the driving rain and near darkness.

"I'm going upstairs to change," said Charlotte, feeling increasingly uncomfortable in her damp clothing. "Then I'll make us a drink." She paused. "Perhaps my father would lend you his nightgown while we dry your clothes by the range in the kitchen."

Adam vigorously shook his head, preferring his wet maroon ruffle shirt and beige trousers to dry on him. He believed his future father-in-law wasn't entirely happy with his daughter's choice for a husband, and didn't want to prevail on her parent for any favours.

An awkward silence fell between the two men, filled by a howling burst of wind driving a sharp rattle of hailstones against the shop window and reverberating down the hallway. Another lightning flash lit the back yard window, quickly followed by a thunder blast that shook the cottage. Flames in an oil lamp perched on the table and two on the sideboard flickered with the vibration.

"This really is a storm and a half," remarked Charlotte's father, prompted into speaking by the adverse weather.

"Are you sure you don't want to change out of those wet clothes?" He made an overture towards hospitality.

Adam declined the offer, deciding that he'd stay for a hot drink, then dash back to the shelter of Mrs Barnaby's cottage where he could change.

Lightning now streaked frequently, followed by crashes of thunder that made it feel as if the shop was under attack.

"Must have struck something very close," said Charlotte's father, picking up a clay pipe from the table.

"You can call me by my first name, Jack, if you wish," the man offered another sociable gesture to his future son-in-law. Charlotte re-appeared in a layered amber dress before Adam could acknowledge the concession.

"Tea for everyone?" she asked, preparing to leave for the kitchen. The men nodded. Jack indicated for Adam to sit in an armchair facing his own at the fireside, then picked up a tinder box on the table to light his pipe.

Shouting outside broke into the room. Jack rushed down the hall towards the noise at the front. Adam followed with Charlotte soon arriving.

Through the shop window overlooking the high street they could see men, women and children running around in blind panic. Jack opened the front door and stepped outside followed by Adam and Charlotte.

"What's happening?" Jack shouted as people ran past.

"The sea's smashing up the piers, ships and boats flying everywhere," a man's voice came through the shouting. As he spoke, a bright lightning flash zigzagged from the deep grey above, striking the roof of a cottage opposite and blasting shattered slate fragments on to fleeing villagers below.

The downpour eased briefly into lighter rain, but better visibility presented new horror.

Jack, Adam and Charlotte stood transfixed as they looked towards the slope leading down to the seafront. Normally it was out of view from this height on the curve. Now they could see huge waves rising and crashing only a stone's throw distance away, with mangled chunks of boat wood being thrown about on the crests like corks.

"Get out!" yelled Jack, "the whole damn place is going." He realised the ground was unstable, and while collapsing it acted like a ramp for the violent storm waves to flood the village.

Adam and Charlotte turned to run, but caught sight of Jack returning inside the shop. The couple quickly followed.

"What are you doing?" Charlotte screamed at her father as he ran towards the back room.

"Fetching our money from the safe. We don't want to end up penniless." Within a few moments he re-emerged holding a leather pouch.

The trio headed towards the open front door. Leading them, Adam suddenly slammed the door shut. The expressions of surprise on Jack and Charlotte's face soon turned to dread realisation. Out of the window they saw a huge wave lobbing large fragments of boat wood as it swept along the street. They threw themselves on the floor to avoid the impact.

With a loud crash, the crest smashed into the window, bursting through the glass with its cargo of wreckage and flooding the room feet deep in writhing seawater. As the monstrous wave receded, it revealed all three drenched and scattered apart on the floor by the turbulent currents. Boots and shoes swept from broken shelves joined the rubble filled chaos all around them.

For a moment Jack and Adam remained still, unsure if the immediate danger had passed. Then they stirred and struggled to their feet. Pain from debris impact racked their bodies, but escape was imperative.

"Charlotte!" the men cried, seeing she wasn't moving.

"I'm alright...just dazed," she replied to their great relief. They helped her up, noticing blood trickling down the side of her neck from glass fragment cuts.

"Come on, we've got to get out!" yelled Adam. They tripped across the rubble to the door, where new horror met them.

Its its ebb, the wave had left bodies of villagers scattered on the street outside. They could also see just short distance away that cottages and the inn lining the road had all collapsed beneath the waves. A flash of lightning highlighted the destruction.

They were about to run when Charlotte realised her father was clutching the door frame for support.

"What's wrong?" she cried.

"Something's hurting my leg. It was okay just now, but I twisted it getting to the door. I'll be fine shortly, so get away and I'll catch you up," he beckoned his daughter and Adam to leave. They hesitated.

"I'll carry you," insisted Adam.

"No, I'll catch you up in a minute." The man didn't want to burden them. Speed was essential.

"Go!" he ordered, knowing full well his leg was broken and he was doomed. It just wouldn't support him, and delay would only endanger the couple.

Reluctantly they ran, Charlotte truly believing that her father would soon be able join them. Adam thought otherwise, but Charlotte's safety was his priority.

It was only seconds later that another giant wave swept along the street, the shop and cottages on each side of the stretch collapsing into the heartless fury.

Charlotte looked behind and stopped running, stunned by the realisation her father had perished. Adam tried to console her, persuade her that both of them would also die if they stayed. She walked back a little, hanging on to the hopeless belief that perhaps she would see the shop intact as the wave drew back. A miraculous survival.

Adam decided he would have to carry her away. Against her will if necessary. The shop and her father were gone. But soon she came to terms with the reality and turned to run again. Suddenly she felt the ground beneath her feet starting to shake. Adam was just in front when he heard her cry out.

"Help me!"

He looked behind. Charlotte was losing her balance. He saw the ground under her crumbling and starting to give way.

"Help me Robin, for God's sake help me!"

He reached out, stretching his arm to pull her upwards as she began to fall away in the landslip. Their fingers touched, but Charlotte tumbled back, rapidly disappearing with the ground as it cascaded into the depths.

Adam had no time to wonder why she'd called him Robin, or to lament his loss. Snaking quickly towards him the unstable ground snatched at his feet and began to draw him down. He spun round and fell forward to clutch at firm surface yet remaining, desperately trying to haul himself clear. But that too had started to yield in the onslaught. Seconds later he joined Charlotte in the depths, tonnes of soil and stones descending over him to enter the sea's new domain.

******

TWO teenage boys strolled along the edge of the seashore. The tide was out and waves lapped gently on to the shale. The youngsters stopped to poke a stick into a translucent jellyfish trapped by the ebbing waters. Content it would never enter the sea alive again, they moved on.

Early morning sunlight highlighted an odd shape further back from the shore and intrigued the pair. They approached, passing the familiar sight to locals of a few remaining stone blocks that once rose to form the seafront wall of Coatehaven village, now long ago reclaimed by the sea.

The boys drew back in surprise as they realised the mangled shape was a human body. They weren't going to poke at that with the stick.

"We'd better tell the police," they uttered together. Not having their phones, they ran towards a steeply winding path at the side of the bay to find the nearest house.

******

FATE was not on Josie's side. Her car developed engine trouble halfway through the journey. The only bit of luck was a lay-by she managed to steer into as the vehicle violently shuddered to a halt. An impatient driver, needing to slow down behind, gave a horn blast passing by.

Josie switched off the engine and rang the car rescue service. She knew a little about the workings of a car engine, but the shudder indicated something more serious could be wrong than just a simple fix. An hour later the service man diagnosed a problem with the drive shaft and the car would need to be transported to a local garage.

Being a Sunday, and with staff shortage problems her rescue provider could only a supply a courtesy car the following day. Her policy covered an overnight stay in a hotel if needed. She rang David. He offered to come and take her home, but she was determined to visit Adam. Something troubled her about his situation. She decided to stay overnight in a local hotel.

Next day Josie pulled up in the courtesy car outside Adam's cottage. She got out and was about to approach the front door when she caught sight of police cordon tape blocking entry to a section of cliff a little further along the coastline. Several patrol cars and an ambulance were parked nearby. Curiosity made her walk towards the scene, joining a group of onlookers.

A police officer appeared, emerging from a path to the shale beach below.

"There's nothing here for you to see," he told the crowd, sounding slightly breathless from the climb. "Please go back to your homes."

The group reluctantly began to depart, talking among themselves.

"They've found a body on the beach," Josie overheard a conversation. At that a surge of fear shot through her.

'Was it Adam?' The vision of him walking towards the cliff edge with the children came to mind. Had he toppled over?

Josie walked back and approached the police officer who now stood guard at the path entrance.

"Is there a body on the beach?" she asked him straight.

"Couldn't say," he replied, "now please move on."

"I think it might be my husband," she persisted, guessing from his non-committal reply that there was a body.

The man's lofty attitude disappeared.

"You'd better speak to my senior officer."

CHAPTER 10

"WHY do you think the body on the beach is your husband?" Detective Inspector, Rachel Ingram asked, sitting opposite Josie at a desk in the police station.

Josie explained that Adam had bought the cottage near the cliff and how he began to behave oddly, his unkempt appearance and seeming to live in a fantasy world.

"He appeared to believe that the old fishing village of Coatehaven had re-appeared from the sea and still existed," she told the detective.

"He even tried to take our son and daughter there, but thank God I managed to stop him before they all fell over the cliff." Josie shivered at the memory. "I fear he may have finally stepped off the edge in his fantasy."

The officer jotted an entry in the laptop on her desk.

"We'll have to wait for the official examination, but if it is your husband I must tell you that you'd have great difficulty in physically identifying the body," the woman softened her tone sympathetically. "It's as though the victim had been beaten and compressed all over by a heavy weight. It could have been earth, stones or rock impacting, but there's been no landfall there for many years."

"Wouldn't those injuries account for a fall from the cliff?" asked Josie.

"A straight fall from the cliff would cause major trauma injury on the impact side, but less on the sides where it might roll," the detective explained. "These injuries are consistently all over. And the victim was found too far from the cliff to have fallen over the edge, even if the body had rolled." She paused, glancing at the laptop. "It's very strange."

Josie closed her eyes, as if attempting to blot out the situation, hoping the body wasn't Adam. Her affection for him still ran deep even though they'd parted.

"The only thing we can more clearly identify is a butterfly tattoo on the left arm," the officer revealed, looking up from the laptop.

Josie closed her eyes again as memory flooded back of the time she and Adam were on holiday in Rome just before they married. They were drinking together one lunchtime on a restaurant patio, when a butterfly settled on her left shoulder. When they met again that evening, he'd had a butterfly tattooed on his left forearm in a pledge of undying love for her. In her youthful eagerness, she couldn't refuse his offer of marriage.

The detective's words confirmed the worst for Josie. DNA or forensic tests would only reveal what she inwardly now believed to be true. It *was* Adam. She felt tears rising in her eyes. D.I. Ingram waited while Josie took a tissue from her handbag to wipe away the trickle.

With no more identity information available for now, she gave contact details to the officer, then left the station to drive back to the cottage. On the journey, her mind struggled coming to terms with event. The unbelievable reality that she dared not tell the detective. Because to anyone else it would seem unbelievable. Laughable, just like David found it when she told him.

Adam said he was staying at the cottage as the guest of a Mrs Barnaby, Josie recalled. The website she'd researched about the lost village of Coatehaven mentioned a Mrs Barnaby living in a property just beyond the village high street, and that it had survived the landfall.

The article related the loss of the woman's two sons and husband at sea, and how the community had rallied to support her. It went on to detail a number of victims in the landfall disaster, among them a young woman called Charlotte Robson.

Alongside the piece was the sketched image of the woman, drawn by an artist named Robin Nesbitt, a wealthy man from London engaged to Charlotte, and who also perished in the fateful storm. Locals had nicknamed him Paintbrush. The artist had drawn many local views and stayed as a guest at Mrs Barnaby's cottage. The article included a drawing of Nesbitt alongside Charlotte. The website owner surmised it was a self-portrait, and showed the man with a horseshoe moustache.

Josie remembered that Adam had introduced a woman to both her and the children as Charlotte Robson, but they hadn't been able to see her. Perhaps Adam really was able to interact with these ghosts of the past, somehow fully existing in that era as a person. A sort of doppelgänger.

She pulled up in the car outside the cottage and walked to the front door wondering if she'd be able to look around inside. The door was locked. She made her way round to the rear, treading a barely visible paved path overgrown with grass and weeds. A heap of rusty corrugated iron sheets and rotted wood marked the unceremonious memorial to an outhouse that once stood in a corner of the yard.

Josie tried the handle of the rotting back door. It opened and she stepped inside to find herself at the rear of the hallway. The kitchen was a complete tip, much like when she'd last visited, but now there were signs of infestation. Rat or mouse droppings littered the floor, and packets of cereal and a mouldy loaf were gnawed through.

She turned away in disgust and made her way upstairs to Adam's bedroom. Clothes were scattered across the floor and she shook her head at the ridiculous arrangement of the sleeping bag on the old bedspread.

In a corner of the room by the window she saw Adam's artwork folder resting against the wall. Curious to see what he'd drawn, she took out some of the sketches and placed them in a bundle on the floor, kneeling down to view them.

The first few in the collection were of coastlines. Then she saw a seafront drawing followed by the sketch of a cobbled high street lined with cottages and shops. It tallied with a drawing in the website article showing old Coatehaven village.

The next image started her heart racing. The pencil portrait featured a young woman who looked exactly like the Charlotte Robson shown in the online article. Josie gazed at it spellbound. Then she saw the signature at the bottom of Adam's sketch. She frantically checked the signatures on the other sketches. He'd signed all of them Robin Nesbitt. Her heart raced almost into overload. She had already been coming to the conclusion that Adam was possessed by the spirit of this artist. Now it dawned that captured in the possession, he'd died in a supernatural replay of the 1838 Coatehaven disaster.

The signed sketches, and better understanding of his strange behaviour were proof enough for her. Others would doubt it. She wouldn't argue with them. Let their own belief take its course.

As she left the cottage, Josie was unaware of the 50-strong contingent of redcoat soldiers assembled outside on the land leading towards to the cliff edge.

Fearing reprisals, the commander of their military base had summoned the unit to take out the troublesome smuggler cell at Coatehaven once and for all.

But the great storm had rapidly moved inland, and forced them to take overnight shelter in a wood five miles from their target destination. They'd only narrowly avoided losing some of their own numbers in the tempest, with trees toppling around them like matchsticks.

From his horse mount the commander surveyed the huge void along the coastline where Coatehaven had stood. He watched a few stragglers wandering the cliff looking for survivors.

The man felt sympathy for innocents who'd perished in the disaster. But he rejoiced mighty nature had taken vengeance for his party of soldiers who'd never returned to base. Of the fishermen's complicity in slaying them he was certain. Witnessing for himself that the village existed no more, he ordered his men to leave.

Josie took a last look at the overgrown cobblestone road leading to the cliff edge, then climbed into her car and drove away.

OTHER BOOKS BY THE AUTHOR

I hope you enjoyed *The Lost Village Haunting*. If you would like to read more of my books they are listed below and available through Amazon. But first a taste of my novel

CURSED SOULS GUEST HOUSE

IT BEGAN with the prospect of a great summertime holiday in beautiful countryside. It descended into the jaws of hell.

"The Yorkshire Dales, that's where we should go," my wife Helen suggested as we sat together on the sofa in our two-bedroom apartment. She was flipping through pages of a country living magazine, and had opened a page showing outstanding views of rolling green pastures, hills and dales in the lush rural setting.

The photos were a welcoming sight compared to the outlook from our home in Birmingham, overlooking an endlessly busy main road at the front and an industrial estate at the back.

We had a week's summer holiday coming, and had been wondering how to spend the time.

"Well, what do you think Andrew?" she asked, as I looked across at the magazine photos.

"Looks good," I replied, distracted from watching a nature programme on the TV about tigers. "Don't think we'll meet too many of them in the Dales," I said, pointing to the shot of a tiger leaping at a terrified wild boar trying desperately to escape.

At that moment I didn't realise we too would soon become the victims of a terrifying powerful force intent on our destruction, with cunning far beyond any tiger.

"Be serious," Helen slapped me on the shoulder. "Stop watching the television and concentrate," she commanded. "I'm trying to arrange our holiday. Now I think we should do it as a hiking tour."

"Not sure about hiking. I want to rest on holiday. We can see places in the car." The idea of walking miles was not particularly appealing to me.

"You've become overweight since you got the office manager's job at Mason's Engineering. You need to lose some." Helen had mentioned my increasing size before. I realised the hiking idea was a bit of a ruse she'd been working on for a while.

It was alright for her as an instructor at the local keep fit centre, where we'd first met a few years ago. I was admittedly a lot shapelier then, enjoying regular exercise. Being office bound in a couple of jobs since had changed my lifestyle.

"Okay, we'll do a hiking holiday," I relented. Helen smiled, acknowledging my defeat.

A fortnight later we set off for Carnswold village in the Yorkshire Dales, complete with new shorts, tops, backpacks and hiking boots, heading towards bed and breakfast accommodation which Helen had booked as the base for our week stay.

The route I drove narrowed into hedgerow lined country lanes as we neared the property that would serve as our temporary home. Breaks in the hedges gave views across miles of pastures. Farmsteads and cottages dotted across the plain rose in and out of valleys to the hazy horizon.

The road descended along winding bends with woodland on each side, and crossed a river bridge as we entered a small hamlet lined with stone cottages. The road continued a little further alongside the river until we arrived at Sunny-side, the name of our cottage accommodation.

It was a name to fit the surroundings perfectly. Warm sunshine lighting the field on the other side of the sparkling river, and woodland at the top of a hill beyond. The world seemed restfully peaceful.

The enchantment didn't last long.

Carrying our suitcases from the car, we opened the gate on to a small paved front garden and rang the doorbell. A middle-aged woman with a droopy face answered.

"Mrs Meadows?" I asked. She nodded.

"I'm Andrew Swanson and this is my wife Helen."

"You're early," she snapped.

I looked at my watch. We'd arrived half-an-hour earlier than the three o'clock time of arrival Helen had given in the booking.

"I don't know if your room's ready yet. Wait a minute." She closed the door and left us standing outside.

"Great start," I remarked to Helen.

"Give it a minute," she replied, forever the mediator. "We've probably caught her in the middle of getting things ready for guests."

That I could forgive, but the woman's rudeness annoyed me. Several minutes later the door opened again.

"Come on in then," Mrs Meadows waved her head for us to enter. She led us down a gloomy narrow hallway, bearing faded floral wallpaper, to a desk where we signed in.

"Number five on the first floor," our host barked, handing over the keys. "Dinner's at seven thirty," the woman turned and walked away, entering a room further down the hall and closing the door.

I was unaware Helen had booked an evening meal for us as well, but some food laid on in the evening after a long hike seemed a good idea.

Our room looked drab, a deeply scratched chest of drawers, the wardrobe with a door that didn't close properly and bedside tables that wobbled. The en-suite sink was stained and the shower cubicle hadn't been cleaned.

"Let's try and make the best of it," Helen detected my discontent.

So making the best of it, we spent time taking a riverbank stroll into Carnswold village a short distance away. I saw a pub and suggested I wouldn't mind a holiday pint of beer. The suggestion was met with disapproval.

"No," said Helen, "on this holiday you can have tea, coffee, water and soft drinks. Maybe a glass of wine with evening meals if you're good. You're going to get some of that weight off."

Once again I conceded, and we settled on coffee in a cafe a little way along the narrow cottage lined high street, passing a small sub-post office and newsagent on the way.

After coffee and sandwiches for our late lunch, we continued the stroll down a footpath leading into a wood and out across a field, enjoying the sunshine and relaxation before returning to the unwelcoming lodging for dinner.

The meal was awful. I had beef casserole, which possibly contained the rubbery meat of a cow three hundred years old, and Helen's vegetarian sausages resembled compacted sawdust. Tasted like it too, Helen remarked, pushing them aside on the plate with her fork to attempt the pulp of remaining mashed potato and cabbage.

We looked across at a couple of dinner guests also staying at Sunnyside. Their grim faces showed signs of agreement.

After so called dinner we decided on an early night to be fit and ready for our trekking. Helen looked beautiful as she undressed, her lovely soft face and long, light brown hair, was a familiar sight to me in our everyday routine at home, but in new surroundings my feelings of desire seemed to be newly sparked into life.

"I'm so glad we met," I told her, undressing and approaching. She looked lovingly into my eyes. We kissed and slowly descended on to the bed.

"Aaagh!" she cried, pushing me away just as her back settled on the mattress.

"What?"

"There's a bloody great lump in the bed." Helen rolled to one side and pulled back the quilt. Sure enough, a bed spring from the innards beneath the sheet rose like a small hill in the centre. It was certainly an effective passion dampener, perhaps left like it by the joyless guest house owner I thought.

We settled instead on trying to get a good night's sleep, which wasn't easy, sinking into sagging mattress on either side of the spring. We'd chosen the Yorkshire Dales for its hills and valleys, but hadn't expected to find them in our bed. I was not going to tolerate this place for much longer.

In the morning breakfast was served to us by a man we hadn't seen until now. I presumed he was Mrs Meadows' husband. His drooping face and similar age certainly matched hers. Without greeting he slapped down our breakfasts on the table, bacon and egg for me and a bowl of muesli for Helen, devoid of any other eating choice.

I complained to him about the room and the bed.

"This isn't the bloody Ritz you know," he growled in return. Then stormed out mumbling curses under his breath.

"He's right there," I said to Helen.

"We'll buy some food out," she tried to placate me. "We'll be hiking most of the time. Let's enjoy the daytimes."

Setting off for our first hike, annoyances with the accommodation soon melted away as we crossed amazing countryside, passing sheep, cows and horses grazing in lush meadows.

We'd been hiking for a couple of hours when the footpath led us off a field into a narrow lane. A few hundred yards further up the slope of the lane, we came alongside a high black wrought iron gate, tall red-brick walls stretching away on each side.

The name 'Longhurst House' was embedded in gold lettering on a grey plate set in the sidewall. Through the gate railings we could see a wide gravel forecourt, and beyond a magnificent L-shaped three-storey house with bay windows, crowned by a lantern roof at the corner and gables on each side. We stopped to admire it.

"That place must be very old," I remarked to Helen.

"Some parts of it date back to the 1650s," a woman's voice seemed for a moment to come from nowhere. "It's been extended and rebuilt over the years."

The voice took the form of an elderly woman who appeared from behind the side wall to greet us with a smile through the gate railings.

"Would you like to take a closer look at the house?" she invited, inquisitive eyes set in a wrinkled, kindly face. We nodded that we would.

Wearing gardening gloves, she lifted the latch in the middle of the gate and opened one side. We entered.

The woman had a green apron over her black dress. She removed the gloves and tucked them into the apron's broad front pocket.

"Just doing a bit of gardening," she said. A grass verge with a colourful flowerbed behind ran along one side of the gravel forecourt. On the other side, a lawn split by a paved path fronted the entrance to the house. The red-brick wall, at least fifteen feet high, surrounded the property.

"My family's lived in this house for three generations," the woman told us with pride. "Come and take a look inside if you wish." She led us along the path towards the front door.

"On a hiking holiday are you?" she obviously guessed from our clothing.

"Attempting to get my husband fit again," Helen joked. The woman smiled.

"Silly me, I'm forgetting my manners. I'm Millicent Hendry," the lady introduced herself as we reached the door. "My friends call me Millie, not that I have so many of them now as most of them have died with the passing years. Feel free to call me Millie."

In return I introduced Helen and myself.

Millie opened the sturdy wooden door and beckoned us inside. The entrance hall looked majestic, painted in deep dark red, with ornate coving and half-length wood panelling along the walls. She opened a door into the lounge displaying framed paintings of scenic Yorkshire Dales pastures, a carved wood surround fireplace and valuable looking Georgian chairs.

Another door opened into the lounge, also featuring a carved wood surround fireplace, a large oriental rug, brown leather sofa and a couple of armchairs. More scenic paintings hung on the walls.

At the end of the hallway a glass panelled door looked over the back garden, another wide gravelled area bordered by beds of shrubs and colourful flowers. A door to the side opened on to the kitchen, which was in complete contrast to the traditional setting we'd seen so far. Inside was a modern cooking range, cupboards and work surfaces.

"Health and Safety laws and all that," Millie said apologetically, noticing our surprise at the difference in style. "I used to do bed and breakfast. The old kitchen, flagstone floor, larder and wood burning stove couldn't meet modern legal standards. So a lot of the original has been replaced or covered over for some years now."

Helen and I shook our heads sympathising at Millie's sad parting with the past.

"Pity you don't do bed and breakfast now," I said, lamenting the fact that such a friendly person and wonderful place was unavailable as an alternative to the dump guest house where we were lodging. As I said it, Helen discreetly tugged my arm as if she wanted me to stop going further down that line.

"Well I get the occasional hikers calling to ask if bed and breakfast is available here," Millie replied. "If I like the look of them, sometimes I'm prepared to put them up for a while. Gives me a bit of company since my husband passed away ten years ago."

"I suppose we'd better be making our way back now," said Helen. "We've more walking to do before we return to our lodging and freshen up for dinner."

It was not exactly a welcoming prospect returning to Sunnyside, and heaven knows what foul food awaited for our evening meal, but Helen was right. As we made our way back to the front door, I told Millie about the terrible place where we were staying. We left the house and began walking along the garden path to the forecourt.

"In no way would I wish to interfere with your plans, but if you like, you're very welcome to come and stay here with

134

me for the rest of your holiday," Millie offered. "I can provide breakfast and evening meals, and I have a lovely bedroom that I think you'd find very comfortable."

For me that seemed like an offer we couldn't refuse. Helen's less than enthusiastic face didn't appear so keen.

"Well, we've paid for the place where we're staying," she said. That was true. Because we'd booked at short notice we had to pay full price up front.

"We'll go back and demand a refund," I insisted, turning to Helen. "The place just isn't up to standard for the money."

"I didn't want to cause an argument," Millie intervened. "It wasn't my intention to interfere with your plans."

"You're not. Please don't apologise," I assured her. "I think Helen's just worried about running costs up." My wife gave me a thunderous look as I spoke.

"I'd enjoy your company, that would be enough compensation for the accommodation," said Millie. "My only charge would be for your food, and I can source that at low cost from a local supplier who I've known for years."

I was sold on the offer. Helen seemed to reluctantly agree.

"We'll stay one more night at our lodging and come over to you tomorrow morning if that's okay?" I asked to Millie.

"Perfectly fine," she agreed.

As we stood talking on the forecourt, a man appeared at the open gate holding two alsatians on leads. The dogs saw us and started barking aggressively.

"Quiet!" Millie ordered, with amazing forceful authority for a woman of her age it seemed to me. The animals immediately obeyed, looking almost guilty for making a noise.

"Those are my precious dogs, Rufus and Petra," Millie announced.

The man holding them on the leashes closed the gate behind him and released the animals. They ran to Millie and she bent down to stroke them The dogs looked thrilled to be in the company of their mistress.

Helen grabbed my arm. She was nervous of strange dogs, and large ones like alsatians in particular. A dog had attacked her when she was a girl she'd told me. It left an indelible fear in her psyche. I put my arm round her shoulders to reassure her all was well. Millie noticed Helen's reaction.

"It's okay. They won't hurt you," she added to my reassurance. "They are very obedient, and they know any guests of mine are my friends to be treated with the utmost respect."

As the dogs wandered off towards the back garden, the man who'd brought them here drew near.

"This is my grandson Nicholas, or Nick as we call him," Millie introduced the newcomer. The man was huge. Tall, muscular and wide, wearing a light blue short-sleeved shirt, and navy trousers.

He nodded to our presence saying nothing, just studying us through curious wide eyes set in a large square face, topped by black curly hair.

"Nick takes the alsatians for a walk now and then," Millie continued telling us about her grandson. "And to dog training sessions every Saturday morning in the village, don't you Nick?" she prompted. The man nodded again. It appeared he was not a great talker.

"There's some homemade blackberry and apple crumble in the kitchen I've made for you," she told him. The news brought a smile to the man's face. He left, heading into the house.

"Forgive Nick, he doesn't say much, but has a heart of gold," Millie explained. "His mother, my daughter, and her husband died in a tragic car crash when he was a boy. I don't think he's ever truly got over the trauma. I brought him up and now he leads a fairly independent life working for a local builder. He has a flat in Oxton village a couple of miles away."

Helen and I weren't quite sure how to respond. It was such a sad tale. Millie saw our awkwardness.

"You're on holiday. Don't let me weigh you down with long past family woes," she brightened up with a smile. "Shall I see you tomorrow?"

"Definitely," I replied. Helen gave a half-hearted nod.

"I think you'll have a truly memorable time here," said Millie, as we walked towards the gate to leave. In the event, she was truly right.

Making our way back across the pastures to Sunnyside, I asked Helen why she'd tugged my arm when Millie suggested we could stay at her house.

"I don't know," she replied, "just this feeling about the place came over me."

"But Millie's a lovely lady," I said. "It looks a fantastic place compared to the rat hole we're staying in. Good deal on the cost too."

"I know, I know," Helen agreed. "Just a feeling I have, that's all."

Soon Andrew and Helen discover that Millie's welcoming greeting hides a horrifying plot.

Find out what happens next in CURSED SOULS GUEST HOUSE

Available on Amazon

OTHER BOOKS BY THE AUTHOR

EMILY'S EVIL GHOST

Emily haunts a country house where evil comes alive.

DEAD SPIRITS FARM

An abandoned old farmhouse becomes a couple's haunted nightmare.

DEADLY ISLAND RETREAT

Trapped on a remote island with ghosts and horrifying revelations.

DARK SECRETS COTTAGE

Shocking family secrets unearthed in a haunted cottage.

THE SOUL SCREAMS MURDER

A family faces terror in a haunted house.

THE BEATRICE CURSE

Burned at the stake, a witch returns to wreak revenge.

THE BEATRICE CURSE 2

Sequel to the Beatrice Curse

A GHOST TO WATCH OVER ME

A ghostly encounter exposes horrific revelations.

A FRACTURE IN DAYBREAK

A family saga of crime, love and dramatic reckoning.

viewBook.at/FractureInDaybreak

VENGEANCE ALWAYS DELIVERS

When a stranger calls – revenge strikes in a gift of riches.

139

THE ANARCHY SCROLL

A perilous race to save the world in a dangerous lost land.

THE TWIST OF DEVILS

Four short stories of devilish manipulation.

MORTAL TRESPASSES

A mystery call leads to a sect raising the dead.

All available on Amazon

For more information or if you have any questions please email me:
geoffsleight@gmail.com

Visit my website:
https://www.geoffsbookhaunt.com/

Amazon Author page:
www.amazon.com/Geoffrey-Sleight

Twitter: twitter.com/resteasily

Your views and comments are appreciated.

Printed in Great Britain
by Amazon

47952715R00087